They Had No Faces

If they were men, their faces were covered with blank, oval masks of silvery metal.

They were flying above the earth in ever-broadening circles. Tracing that circle to its center, Lux stiffened as he realized the aerial search must have started from the house where he had just spent the night.

Expressionless faces inhumanly blank, dangling stiffly like jointed wooden puppets, the seven Silver Men flashed swiftly through the bright sunlight. There was something cold and menacing in the fixity of their purpose; something ominous in their rapid, swooping flight: they were like men—hunting.

And they were hunting—him!

Time War

Lin Carter

WILDSIDE PRESS

This book is for my old friend **JOE SCHAUMBURGER**
who loves this kind of van-Vogtian puzzle-yarn
as much as I do.

Contents

I. *The Impossible Murderer*

JOHN LUX lifted his eyes from the sheaf of subelectronic specifications he had been studying, and stared directly into the muzzle of a revolver.

The expensively decorated executive suite was untenanted, save for himself. The large room was almost soundless, except for the hum of the air conditioning and the distant chatter of typewriters in the outer offices, beyond the heavy mahogany door. He blinked and looked again, too completely astonished to move, to cry out, or even to think.

In a detached manner, almost as if part of an audience watching an enactment, or an observer looking on as these things happened to someone else, he noted that the gun was a Colt .45 automatic, similar to the one that lay in the bottom drawer of his own desk.

His mind veered giddily away from the element of the impossible. Nevertheless, the gun hung there in mid-air before his desk, suspended in emptiness, without any visible support.

And *that* was craziness; such things did not, could not, happen!

Yet there it was.

Slanting rays of sunlight, shining through the long slats of the venetian blinds that showed through the heavy, half-parted drapes, glittered along the blued steel of the gun barrel. It was not, could not be, an illusion; this was solid. This was real.

A moment ago he had been absorbed in his plant engineers' report on the subelectronic guidance system for a new ICBM prototype missile the government had contracted with his firm to produce. A moment before, the world had been ordinary—prosaic—even a little dull.

Now he was thrust into a living nightmare.

The revolver did not waver in the slightest. It was as rigid as if clenched in the grip of an invisible hand!

These were the thoughts that flashed through his mind in the first half-second as he stared directly into the cold, black, unwinking eye of the pistol barrel.

Then a metallic click rang loudly through the tense stillness of the office. It was as if an invisible finger had clicked off the safety catch. As fascinated as if he were staring into the eye of a cobra, John Lux saw the trigger move ever so slightly. He knew, with the finality of utter conviction, that in the next split second a bullet would go crashing into his brain.

He knew, also, that he could never throw himself aside in time to avoid that bullet.

The room roared with the thunder of a single gunshot—

—and Lux inexplicably found himself standing in the corner of the far wall, thirty feet from his desk, braced on trembling legs, panting and soaked with sweat, as if exhausted by some athletic feat, some physical ordeal of almost superhuman effort.

The room swam about him drunkenly; he seized the back of an expensive Swedish Modern couch to steady himself until the vertigo passed. Mastering his amazement, he looked down at himself, dreading what he might find.

And found—*nothing!*

No blood, no wound. Neither his suit nor his shirt front bore the marks of powder burns. It was as if the entire experience had been some elaborate joke, some enormous hoax. Or as if he had only dreamed the thing, and had not really experienced it in actuality.

But this was madness!   There was no doubt in his mind that what had seemed to happen had really occurred. Lux was a hard-headed man, an electronic scientist, a successful businessman, a powerful industrial magnate. He had clawed his way up from the bottom of the heap, and had reached his present pinnacle of achievement because of his unique and valuable combination of the businessman's practicality and the scientist's imagination. Dreams—magic and mysticism, the occult and the inexplicable—had no room in his life.

He believed in what his senses told him was hard and real, and he had only contempt for fuzzy speculation and dreamy theorizing. Now he was confronted with a situation in which his senses had reported a reality that was impossible—that must, therefore, be empty illusion! For an instant, he toyed with the seductive thought of hallucination; in the next instant, with reluctance, he rejected it.

For the gun *had* fired! No slightest doubt of that fact existed in his mind. The roar of the explosion still rang in his ears; the sharp stench of cordite stung his nostrils.

Swiftly, he glanced across the room to where the pistol had hung in mid-air.

But it was gone!

It had winked out of existence a fraction of a second after it had fired at him.

The faint clatter of typewriters had ceased in the room beyond. A sudden clamor or shrill, questioning voices came faintly to his ear. The door swung open and a young woman in a prim silk dress looked frantically about.

"Sir? Mr. Lux! Are you all right? We heard a—"

Some intuition he did not really understand bade him soothe his secretary's alarm.

"Everything is all right, Miss Forrester. A slight accident. I was cleaning my pistol—the pistol I keep in my desk—and it fired accidentally. I guess I had forgotten it was loaded."

He ushered the young woman out of his office, told her he did not wish to be disturbed, and returned to his desk. Had the whole thing been a dream of some kind? Had he dozed off momentarily, nodded over the technical report, and dreamed the entire incident?

John Lux smiled grimly, and a bit perplexedly. If so, his dreams had a remarkable power to infect others—for Miss Forrester had heard the gunshot, too! That could hardly be the answer.

On a sudden impulse, he unlocked a drawer in the mahogany desk and stared down at the blued-steel barrel of his Colt .45—a relic of his war years.

The reek of cordite, which lingered in the heavy drapes of the room, and hovered in the air above the expensive carpet, was particularly strong here. He reached down and took up the pistol, and froze as amazement lanced through him.

The barrel was hot, stinging his fingertips!

He sniffed the muzzle, then snapped the breech and counted the cartridges. One bullet had been fired, and recently. The conclusion was inescapable . . .

The weapon that had sought his life was his own gun!

Shaken and unnerved by the inexplicable experience, Lux left the office, telling his secretary to cancel all appointments, as he was leaving for the day.

He rode down to ground level in his private express elevator and strode out through the marble-paved lobby of the Lux Building and into the street. He could have called for his chauffeur, but he felt like walking. Fresh air and sunshine might clear his head.

The nearest bar was across the street, on the far corner of the block. He felt in such a dazed, bewildered mood that perhaps an ice-cold Martini would do him good. He strode through the early afternoon crowd to the corner, waited for the traffic light to change, and started across.

Some vague premonition, perhaps a blur of sudden movement at the periphery of his vision, made him glance suddenly over his shoulder.

Although the light was still green and the traffic stood immobile, waiting for the pedestrians to cross, one car had surged suddenly into motion. It was one of the new turbo cars, a huge, glittering machine, and it was bearing down at him with whirling speed.

The pedestrians to either side broke in a panic and scattered. But Lux stood as if rooted to the pavement, unable to move, unable even to think.

Like a gleaming, enormous projectile, the huge vehicle flashed toward him, swelling to gigantic proportions. In an instant his broken, mangled body would be slammed aside, flying through the air, to crash against the pavement, oozing crimson. He could not possibly leap clear; the car was almost on top of him; another instant and—

—he found himself suddenly on the sidewalk, clutching a lamppost, streaming with perspiration from every pore!

Raising his eyes, he saw the huge, gleaming turbo car race through the empty space his body had occupied a fraction of second before.

Cries and shouts of alarm sounded all about him, and the shrilling of a police whistle, the squeal of brakes. He shut his eyes, suddenly faint, and opened them as a huge hand clamped on his arm in a tight grip. A police officer, red-faced, stared at him.

"My God, it's Mr. Lux! That was a close call—I could have sworn you were a goner—crazy hit-and-run maniac!" The officer broke off, red face puzzled. "But how did you jump out of the way in time! I could have sworn you—are you all right, sir? Shall I call an ambulance?"

Lux swallowed, and forced his will down like an iron vise on his trembling body.

"No—no need for that, Officer—thanks, but what I need right now is a drink!"

The interior of O'Leary's was cool and dark, and it smelled of leather upholstery and expensive cigars. He chose a secluded table in a dark corner and gulped down a bitterly cold Martini and lit a cigarette, drawing the blue smoke deep into his lungs, letting it out slowly.

He supposed he was a brave man, but two attempts

on his life within the span of thirty minutes is enough to shake up anyone! Ordering a second drink, he sat there and let the tension drain out of him slowly.

No businessman can rise as high as Lux, and as fast, without making enemies. Surely he had made a few. Not yet forty, he was at the helm of a giant industrial complex, with a finger in half a hundred pies. No doubt there were enough business rivals around who wished him in his grave!

For that matter, he held several top-secret defense contracts, too. There was that mysterious what-is-it they were putting together out in Farmersville—the robot nuclear missile. Half a dozen foreign powers would love to get their hands on the specifications for the missile—and would probably settle for having him put out of the way, and the corporation thrust suddenly into receivership, thus putting an end to the missile project.

But—no, neither business rivals nor international espionage was behind these mysterious assaults on his life, of that he was certain. For both of the mysterious attacks had savored of the inexplicable—the weird—even the occult. No visible murderer had leveled that pistol at his brain. And as for the incident of the turbo car, well, there had been an eerie shadow of the unknown cast across that incident, too. For as he had clung to the lamppost, watching the murder car hurtle through the vacancy where his body had been only a split second before, he had gotten a clear look into the driver's seat.

And there had been no driver.

No one at all had been riding in the car that had tried to kill him!

Finishing his second drink, John Lux used the phone in the back of the bar and called for his chauffeur. A few minutes later a long black limousine pulled up, and Lux got in. The air conditioning was cool and tangy; the car glided into the stream of traffic.

Lux rubbed his brow, thinking. Today was Friday. The weekend lay ahead of him. He had planned to stay in his East Side town house this weekend, and had thought to call Marlene and make a date for dinner. But he felt too jumpy, too distraught. Suddenly, for some reason, he thought of Dr. Havering. It had been many months since he had last visited the older man, who had been one of his professors at college. A rare understanding had sprung up between the two men, so very different in age, in experience, even in temperament. Havering was the perfect companion for his mood; Lux felt a deep urge to discuss the inexplicable events of the day with some intelligent, first-class mind, to talk things out.

He remembered, too, and with a growing sense of excitement, that while Dr. Havering's chosen field was in the area of behavioral psychology, he had for many years held a special interest in the odd, the uncanny, the inexplicable—the sort of "Fortean" phenomena which was known to occur, but which fitted none of the theories or laws of orthodox science. With Havering, he felt assured of a sympathetic ear and a mature understanding.

The Doctor, he recalled, had retired from teaching some years before, and lived in a secluded house on the edge of the city. Yielding to an irresistible impulse, Lux took up the interphone and directed his driver to pull over to the curb. He got behind the wheel, handed the man a twenty-dollar bill and told him to take a taxi home, and pulled away from the curb, leaving his chauffeur staring after him in puzzlement.

The long drive out of the city gave Lux an opportunity to relax. Sunset painted the west with its crimson as Lux pulled off the highway into a private side road, traced a long curve past rows of great oaks, and pulled up before a large old house, all warm red brick, creamy stucco, and dark wood.

Havering's man servant, a Filipino named Komo, answered the doorbell and admitted Lux into a dark hall. Heavy antique furniture gleamed with polished wax in the dim light; an excellent Persian carpet was luxuriously soft underfoot. In a moment the silent little man returned to lead Lux into the library, where the older man awaited him.

Havering had a tanned, lean face with aristocratic features and fine, intelligent eyes under a wide brow and smooth silver hair. He wore dark slacks and a black velvet smoking jacket.

"John, how splendid to see you again. What a nice surprise, your dropping in unexpectedly like this! Of course, you'll stay for dinner . . . ?"

John Lux grinned. "I'll stay the night, if you have no objections."

"Objections! I'm delighted; it'll give us a chance to have a good long talk. Come in—sit down—have a brandy and soda. You look fagged out. Working hard these days?"

"Hardly working, rather. The corporation literally runs itself." Lux sat back in the comfortable embrace of the huge leather armchair and stretched his long legs out before the cheery fire that snapped and crackled in the fieldstone grate. Havering put a glass in front of him, took a seat himself, and began to stoke up a battered briar pipe. For a moment Lux just sat there, soaking up the warm atmosphere of the large, high-ceilinged room. Fine leather bindings stood in rows on the mahogany shelves; sunlight gleamed ruddily through the tall French windows. Marble-topped tables, cluttered with rare pieces of Chinese cloisonné, carvings of ivory, amber, and jade, scholarly journals and newspapers, lay about in the rich gloom.

Then he began to talk. He described both attempts on his life in an unemotional, dryly factual tone, being careful to remember and relate every detail with all the precision and clarity possible. As for the older man, he sat quietly, smoking, listening intently, not interrupting. When Lux finished, he sat back while Havering cleared his throat and rubbed the bridge of his nose thoughtfully.

"You've obviously come to me because of my study of such phenomena," the Doctor observed. "Well . . . I've collected notes on such things for years—Fort's books are full of them, of course. But I don't have any pat answers, any neat theories, readily to hand."

"Just what *do* you think, then?" Lux asked.

"Well, there are several obvious explanations that spring easily to mind—although I'd say we can rule them all out in your case. I know you too well to suggest that you are mentally deranged; your lifelong habits make it a virtual impossibility that you were drunk on alcohol or on some kind of narcotic and merely hallucinated both occurences; and the eyewitnesses in both events, your secretary, who heard the gunshot, and the police officer, who saw the car try to run you down, rule out the possibilities of it all being just a dream—unless your witnesses themselves are part of the dream.

"No . . . let's consider that everything you have related to me this evening actually occurred, and just as you have described it. Someone—some person or organization, or some force—seems to want you dead. Any ideas who?"

Lux related his earlier suspicions regarding business rivals and foreign espionage, as well as his arguments against either of those elements being the power behind the enigmatic murder attempts.

Dr. Havering nodded thoughtfully. "Yes, it seems wildly improbable that General Nucleodynamics or Red China is out to murder you by means of voodoo or black magic! If such forces wanted to take your life badly enough to make an actual attempt on it, there are plenty of perfectly ordinary, mundane methods they would employ first, before turning to the occult."

He suddenly shot a keen, appraising glance at Lux.

"You know, John, there's one aspect to these phenomena we have not touched upon."

"What's that?"

"The methods of murder are certainly occult enough—but what about your peculiar way of avoiding death? You spoke of finding yourself instantaneously transported the length of your room, thus evading the gunshot—and a similar feat of teleportation carried you to the farther side of the street, snatching you from under the wheels of the hurtling automobile. Now *this* is something I perhaps know a little about! Teleportation is a known phenomenon, and the literature is filled with documented cases of individuals who have possessed the ability."

"Teleportation? I've heard the word, but I know nothing about the occult," Lux said. Havering shook his head.

"Teleportation is not in the least occult," he said firmly. "It's akin to the extrasensory faculties Rhine and his colleagues have studied for years at Duke. A paranormal motive power by which, in moments of stress, certain rare individuals are able to transport themselves, or exterior objects, across space instantaneously."

Lux shrugged. "Sounds occult enough to me, Doc!"

"Nevertheless, there is nothing supernatural about it; it belongs to the province of paraphysics—the actions of an unknown force whose dynamics we have yet to figure out. Someday the math boys will have it all down in solid equations, just how and why it works. But right now, it's still a mystery. And—have you forgotten, John?—*this is not the first time you have teleported!*"

Havering's phrase triggered a memory that had slept in Lux's mind for years. The instant the Doctor mentioned it, the memory came flooding back . . . more than fifteen years before, when a young tank commander serving in Korea, his vehicle had been trapped in a barrage of enemy mortar fire. An instant before their tank was blown to smithereens by a direct hit through the hatch, Lux's observer had yelled a warning . . . a warning cut in half by a deafening explosion and a blinding flash of white fire . . . and Lux had blacked out momentarily, awakening to find himself knee deep in the muddy waters of a rice paddy, *half a mile away*, and well out of the danger zone.

The incident could easily have been explained away as a case of shell shock; half conscious, Lux could have staggered away from the wrecked tank, not recovering consciousness until he was well away from the scene of the explosion. And on such terms he had indeed explained it to his superiors when he had rejoined his unit. No one in the world, except himself and Dr. Havering, to whom he had told the story, knew his proof that such had not and could not have been the explanation.

For at the precise moment the artillery observer had yelled out his warning—an instant before the tank had shattered apart under the devastating impact of a direct hit by a mortar shell filled with powerful explosives—*Lux had just happened to be glancing at his watch.*

And when he had come to himself, to find he somehow stood up to his knees in the cold, muddy waters of a rice paddy, he was still engaged in the act of looking at the dial.

In the fraction of a second before the explosion had wrecked the tank, the second hand had been sweeping toward a numeral. Standing there with water seeping up his fatigues and soaking into his combat boots . . . *the hand was still sweeping up to the same numeral!*

It was only later, when he had oriented himself, and had learned that he had reappeared a good half-mile from his former position, that the full enigma of the experience came to him with all its brain-stunning implications.

Somehow, miraculously, he had traversed half a mile of space in an interval of time too minuscule to be measured by his watch!

How?

To this day he had never found the answer to that question.

II. *The Lady Lis*

JOHN LUX came awake suddenly, and for a moment he could neither identify the slight sound that had aroused him from sleep nor recognize his surroundings.

Then it came back to him . . . the puzzling events of the previous day, the drive to Dr. Havering's house on the outskirts of the city, their conversation, and the weird, baffling conclusion they had tentatively arrived at—teleportation.

Komo had served them a superb gourmet dinner. Jonas Havering was a stimulating dinner companion, a brilliant conversationalist, a fountain of coruscating wit and ribald anecdote, and a rich fund of literary allusion. Lux had thoroughly enjoyed himself, and had drunk a bit more of the fine vintage wine than he perhaps should have—finishing the evening rather too late to drive back to his town house. The Doctor had asked Komo to open one of the seldom-used guest rooms for him, insisting that Lux spend the night.

Having donned a pair of the Doctor's spare pajamas, he had retired, only to find it difficult to sleep. His mind a buzzing turmoil of theory and conjecture, he had lain awake a long time, staring at the ceiling, thinking.

Somehow, after a while he drifted slowly into a shallow, uneasy slumber, broken by vivid and menacing dreams.

What had awakened him? He lay rigid, conscious of the warm comfort of the huge double bed, of the darkness and cool silence of the room, wondering what it could have been that had jerked him so abruptly into wakefulness.

Then it came again—that faint, stealthy rustle of sound across the room.

He turned his head on the pillow, staring through the blackness toward the half-open window, where heavy drapes, tightly drawn, held the silver moon at bay, save for a vagrant sliver of pallid, brilliant light.

And, as he looked, John Lux saw a moving shape of darkness as it obscured that one sharp line of clear radiance.

Cold perspiration burst out on his body, which was clad only in the light sleeping garments.

Something had moved in the silent room. Something was moving between his bed and the window beyond.

The conclusion was unnerving, but terrifyingly obvious.

Another person beside himself was in the room. *Some unknown intruder was creeping through the darkness toward him!*

Lux had lived a hard, action-filled life, and had known danger and violence. He was a big man, deep-chested, tall, with heavily muscled shoulders, well able to handle himself in any kind of physical encounter. He tensed, steeling himself for confrontation with a burglar who might well be armed. Then, without a sound, moving carefully so as to give no warning, Lux reached across and switched on the lamp that stood on a small table beside the bed. The room was bathed in soft light, and to his surprise, Lux saw that the midnight intruder was—a woman! A young woman, darkly attractive, with alert, intelligent eyes in a cool, aristocratic face. Her slim figure was encased in a curious, tight-fitting one-piece garment of some darkly glittering fabric he could not recall having seen before.

She had been approaching the side of his bed in the dark. Now she stood tensely, blinking against the light which had unexpectedly flooded the room.

He relaxed a bit. The mysterious young woman was not armed, and he seemed in no immediate danger. In a loud voice, he demanded to know what she was doing there.

"I have no time to answer questions, John Lux," the woman said swiftly, in a warm contralto voice. "I must ask you to listen very carefully to what I shall tell you. Already, there have been two deliberate attempts to take your life—"

"How do you know that?" he asked bluntly.

She shook her head impatiently, long dark hair tousling.

"Be silent and pay attention! It requires an enormous expenditure of energy to sustain my presence in this segment of reality. And if you are to survive the next scheduled attack on your life, you must possess certain information which only I can give you."

"Very well, I'm listening."

"That's better! Now you must listen carefully to what I am going to tell you, for your survival—your very life—depend on your grasp of the fundamentals of the situation. You may think of me as the Lady Lis, if you like. I am not a native of your world, or of your century at all. I inhabit an alternate reality-segment of the very distant future, perhaps one million years from your own epoch. My era is known as the Arcadian Age, and represents the ultimate development of human civilization. But our reality segment is imperiled—"

Lux felt confused.

"What do you mean by 'reality segment'?" he asked. She frowned impatiently.

"You must not interrupt—every moment is precious! Surely, even the savants of your primitive age must be aware that from every major Crisis Point—every really significant point of decision in time—alternate paths of future history branch off?"

Lux hazily remembered once idly leafing through a book of such nature, speculations of what "alternate realities" might have developed had Alexander the Great not died in Babylon of pneumonia but lived to consolidate his conquests and to organize his empire; had Napoleon broken Wellington at Waterloo and swept on to invade and conquer England; had Hitler's scientists developed the atom bomb before the Manhattan Project and used the new weapon in his robot bombs to destroy London, Washington, Moscow, and New York. He nodded, hesitantly; the intense young woman swept on.

"Very well! Our world of the Arcadian Age is one such alternate branch of time. Its very existence is contingent upon a historical event which, according to our histories, occurred about two hundred thousand A.D.—to employ the curious chronological system used in your own era. This pivotal event is the destruction of Arthex the Living City, which liberated mankind from its gilded prison and forced our ancestors into the wilderness, where they learned to survive, rediscovering courage, endurance, and resourcefulness. Your enemy—the man striving to kill you—is known as Malaire. He is the master of the Living City, and the last great despot of the Urban Age, as the era is know. Malaire's regime, *circa* two hundred thousand A.D., was a dead end for human civilization, and his overthrow liberated mankind into the Arcadian Age. But we Arcadians inhabit only one of several alternate realities: one is a dead, barren world, in which the last of Urban Age men dwindled and died out, and civilization came to an end; the other, a hideous metal world of robot intelligence, and there, too, mankind became extinct following the Urban Age."

Her handsome features were pale and tense, her flashing eyes eloquent of despair.

"Each of these alternate reality-segments has an equal Probability Potential of becoming 'actual history.' Recently our sages have determined that the Crisis Point—the destruction or continuance of the Living City—is too nebulous for absolute certainty; it was resolved that we must influence and shape the flow of events in what is, to us, remote antiquity, to insure that Arthex indeed falls, as related in our histories."

Lux's mind felt numb; this mass of nearly incomprehensible information bewildered him.

"Wait a minute," he protested. "You're going too fast for me! What is this thing you call a 'living city,' and what's wrong with it that it should be destroyed, and—most of all!—what does all this have to do with me?"

"To answer your questions in detail would consume more time than I possess," the mysterious future-woman replied. "However: Arthex is the last center of civilization on the planet in the year two hundred thousand A.D. It is the fortress and refuge to which the surviving remnants of mankind fled after the ruinous and exhausting City Wars devastated most of the land surface of the planet. It is a gorgeous congeries of luxurious and frivolous buildings, constructed for pure pleasure. The City is the last of its kind, the ultimate end product of two hundred thousand years of urban evolution, and it resembles a vast playground where the surviving remnants of mankind dwell in safety, coddled and entertained and protected by a super-electronic brain. This mechanical mind, this artificial intelligence, maintains the life-support systems, controls the robot factories, supervises the lives of the last men. The Living City is a closed environment, a huge playpen in which all that survives of mankind remains isolated from the wilderness of the outside world, insulated against reality, shielded from danger and suffering—and also from bravery, ingenuity, determination, and strength—survival factors rapidly being bred out of the race. The Living City is one giant machine for pleasure, and it must fall if mankind is not to dwindle into self-extinction. Save for the City and its machine brain, all of the rest of the planet has returned to primal wilderness. In order for mankind to evolve further, it must break free of the controlled environment of Arthex and move into the wilderness."

Lux shook his head. "I still do not see why!"

She tossed her head impatiently.

"Because the race is over-protected, coddled and

babied by the City! Men are becoming accustomed to the comforts of the City, and the urge to explore, to risk danger, to endure discomfort, to pioneer, is being bred out of the race, and will soon vanish entirely!"

"What role does Malaire play in all of this?" he asked.

"We are not entirely certain," the Lady Lis confessed. "The City and he maintain some sort of alliance between them. He is a mysterious individual, and our researchers have not been able to discover his origins. One theory is that he is an immortal, and that it was he who designed the Living City in the first place."

"All right, then, another question. Why does he want to destroy me?"

"Because he thinks you pose a threat to him, and are a potential enemy of the City. Let me explain. Ten thousand years ago—before my own time, that is—we launched a robot destroyer into the Arthex reality segment. The device is an enormous aerial fortress with an artificial intelligence; it has become known to the citizens of Arthex as the Weapon Machine. Following the orders programmed into it, as soon as the Machine appeared above the City it began attacking it with energy weapons. But we did not take into our calculations the immense technology stored in the City brain, or its amazing capacity to act swiftly in emergencies that threaten its own survival. Before the Weapon Machine could demolish more than just the periphery of Arthex, the City created the Null Sphere—a region of distorted space which shields the City like a protective dome of force. Within the Null Sphere space has been artificially distorted into a kind of pseudospace wherein the laws of physics no longer apply. Neither energy nor matter can exist within the Null Sphere. That means, of course, that no destructive ray or explosive missile can penetrate the dome of force. Or, to be precise, they can in fact enter it, but once they have done so they cease utterly to exist."

"I gather, then, that the position is one of stalemate," he mused. The girl nodded.

"Precisely: a stalemate that has continued now for ten millennia. Our attempt to destroy Arthex and free mankind from its bondage to the machine mentality which has almost sapped its will has resulted in walling mankind in behind a completely impenetrable barrier."

"And this Weapon Machine you speak of—what has it been doing all this time?"

"Nothing!" she snapped. "The siege has ended in stalemate. The Weapon Machine cannot destroy the City; neither can it depart. It is a mindless, self-powered automation of sheer destructiveness, and once it was launched into the Arthex segment of reality, we lost our ability to control it or to countermand its programming. It single-mindedly continues the siege, which has thus far lasted for ten thousand years, and it will continue it forever!"

"Well, hasn't this mysterious, enigmatic individual, Malaire, or the City itself made any attempt to destroy the Weapon Machine and remove this threat to their existence?"

"Doubtless they would have made some such attempt, but the Null Sphere works both ways, you see. No projectile or ray can penetrate it from outside to destroy the City, and neither can the City send a projectile or ray through the Sphere from the interior to destroy the Weapon Machine."

Lux rubbed his brow, trying to sort out this profusion of data into some sort of pattern.

"We come again to the question of what all of this has to do with me," he observed

"You have yet to discover the fact in your own brief time span," the woman said, "but you are a rare mutation of the common race. The chances were one hundred billion to one of such a mutation occurring, but they did occur. You are a neuro-radionic superman with a nervous system capable of tapping, controlling, and directing energy flow throughout the entire electromagnetic spectrum. This means that at need you can divert any exterior energy source to supply you with power. This was, in time, discovered by Malaire. Anxious to break the deadlock and put an end to the ten-thousand-year siege of Arthex, Malaire discovered, through the logic machines that are a portion of the City Brain, that only once in human history on this planet has such a rare mutation occurred, and that toward the close of the twentieth century. The logic machines also divulged the origins of the robot destroyer we launched against Arthex. Malaire knows, then, that we have the means to project objects and persons across time. The logic machines told Malaire that there was a point-nine-nine four probability factor that his enemies in the Arcadian Age would attempt to enlist your assistance in their war against Arthex. He fears that your rare ability to tap and manipulate energy sources makes you the one human being in all eternity who might be able to interfere with the power that sustains the Null Sphere and protects the Living City from the ravening destructive robot we have pitted against it. Therefore, Malaire seeks to destroy you before we Arcadians can enlist you in our cause."

John Lux was stunned. He blinked, striving desperately to find something to say. As he did so, a humming sound came into the lamp-lit air, and the supple figure of the young woman flickered and dimmed. Her features whitened, her lustrous eyes flashed.

"I am losing contact," she said rapidly. "I can no longer sustain existence in this segment. Listen carefully, we do not have very much time! The next twenty-four hours are crucial. There will be further assaults on your life. If you can survive them, you will be safe, and if not—all is lost! I advise you not to return to the city. Go to another city where you are not so well known—take rooms under an assumed identity—lose yourself in the crowd. And keep hidden—at all costs, you must survive the next twenty-four hours!"

"But!—" he began. She cut him off with an imperious gesture.

"Malaire may use the Silver Men against you," she said. "They are his deadliest killers; watch out for them. Your ability to manipulate energies is still in its instinctual phase, and you do not yet know how to control it, so do not attempt to fight them. Stay hidden and keep out of sight!"

"But what if I—"

"Should you be trapped, and find yourself in a completely hopeless situation, use this." She tossed him a small bright metal object, which he snatched out of the air with an automatic gesture. "Keep this on your person at all times. If the situation becomes hopeless and there is no way out, hold this tube to your ear. It will transport you to a place of safety, where neither Malaire nor the Silver Men are able to hunt for you. But it is only to be used in the last extremity, remember!"

And suddenly she was gone!

Lux stared blankly at the empty space her body had occupied a fraction of a second before. She had snapped out of existence as if she had never been there at all!

He went into the bathroom and bathed his face in cold water. Tingling from the refreshing splash, he stared at his face in the mirror. His smooth, dark, neatly trimmed hair was disarranged; his tanned, square-jawed face was flushed; his cool gray eyes were confused and bewildered. And with good reason!

Simple common sense and practical reasoning told him to dismiss the woman's fantastic tale as hysteria or delusion. It was incredible—worse still, ludicrous—to believe that he was a pawn in an age-long war between strange civilizations of the distant future. And yet . . . and yet there was no question but that some mysterious force sought his destruction. Twice in the past twenty-four hours some supernatural adversary had attempted to take his life. And the attractive young woman who called herself the Lady Lis warned that this was only the beginning!

Staring at his face in the mirror, John Lux asked

himself if it was possible he was going mad. If so, he could dismiss the seeming reality of the bewildering sequence of recent events as merely convincing hallucinations conjured up by his paranoia.

But the face that looked back at him was tanned, clear-eyed, healthy. It was not the hysterical visage of a gibbering maniac. And he recalled that he had spent the evening in the company of Dr. Havering, a behavioral psychologist; surely his host would have noted any of the stigmata of mental derangement if he had displayed them. He was reluctantly forced to conclude that his sanity was unshaken.

If that was so, then the implications were unmistakably that the ridiculous tale the young woman had narrated to him was true in every particular, however much it sounded like some of the wilder plots of science fiction!

And besides, he had a piece of material evidence that what he had seen and spoken to was no hallucination: the bit of bright metal she had tossed to him—the instrument that was supposed to transport him to a safe place if he became hopelessly trapped. He had put it down on the sink; now he took it up and examined it curiously.

It was a thick, smooth tube of some bright metal like chrome, an inch and a half long, slightly less than half an inch wide, and as heavy as if it were made of lead. The metal surface was slick, unbroken, devoid of any features. If this was some sort of transportation device, it must be crammed with ultraminiaturized components, he thought.

Returning to the bedroom, Lux noted the time: six in the morning. On sudden impulse, tucking the tube into his pocket, he put on his clothes, scrawled a hasty note to his host, saying he had decided to go away for a brief rest, and went downstairs quietly so as not to awaken anyone.

Letting himself out the front door, he climbed behind the wheel of his limousine and swung about, driving back the way he had come. Once on the highway, he drove smoothly along, following a northerly route, his mind busy with plans.

Whether or not the young woman's fantastic story was true, the best course to follow might be the one she had suggested: to leave town for a couple of days, losing himself in another city under another name. It seemed hardly likely that his mysterious enemies could trace him wherever he might go.

Havering lived on the edge of town, a twenty-minute drive from the small airport where Lux kept a plane, a small two-seater he used for business trips to nearby industrial centers. He could leave the car in the hangar and be many miles away by mid-morning.

The airfield mechanic had just gone on duty when John Lux pulled the big limousine into the field and halted before his private hangar. The man found nothing out of the usual in Lux's making an early-morning flight, and trundled the small plane out onto the runway while Lux drove his car into the rear of the hangar. The mechanic fueled the plane and agreed amiably when Lux asked him to tell no one of his departure, as he hoped to steal a march on a business rival by an unannounced trip to confer with businessmen in a neighboring city. The twenty-dollar bill that Lux slipped into the man's hand sealed the bargain.

He took off smoothly, circled the field, and headed north. There were several medium-sized cities within a radius of one hundred miles to which he might go. The size of the bill he had used to purchase silence from the mechanic reminded him that he should think about his money needs over the next day or two. He was annoyed to discover less than one hundred dollars in his wallet. That would barely suffice under normal circumstances, but if his flight was to entail any unusual expenses, he might be hampered by lack of funds.

The nearest town in which he maintained a private bank account was Weston, a small manufacturing center some eighty-five miles to the north. As it was the center of several light industries in which Lux maintained a controlling or participatory interest, he kept a cash reserve account in the leading bank, the Weston Trust and Savings, against his occasional need for funds during overnight visits or weekend business conferences.

Thinking it over, he decided on Weston as the best possible hiding place for his requirements. The city was small, but large enough for him to easily lose himself in it, so long as he stayed clear of the various clubs and institutions and hotels he usually patronized during visits. And if his cash supplies ran out, he could always secure funds from his account.

Checking the local and state maps he kept in a small briefcase in the airplane's cabin, he flew steadily north.

And not once did he suspect that he was being followed!

III. *The Silver Men*

John Lux handled the controls with absent, automatic efficiency, his thoughts elsewhere. It was a clear, bright, cool morning. The wind was sharp and fresh, the sky an expanse of pure blue, unmarred by the smallest cloud. The very monotony of the flight gave him the leisure to think over some of the astonishing revelations the futurewoman had told him the night before.

Perhaps the most amazing of these was the notion that he was some kind of rare, unique mutation—a "neuro-radionic superman," the Lady Lis had called him. He was not entirely certain that he understood what this curious term meant. Something to do with the ability of his nervous system to control external energy sources, to tap them for power at need.

He frowned, pondering the implications. Was this the answer to the riddle of his ability to teleport himself out of danger? Dr. Havering had called his talent rare, but had divulged the fact that Fortean literature contained copious, documented instances of such phenomena.

How did that square with the contention of his mysterious early-morning visitor, who had claimed that his was a thoroughly unique mutation? His neuro-radionic powers were the result of a rare genetic accident, she had said; only once in the entirety of human history had such a mutation occurred, and he was the one.

Havering's contention was at odds with Lis's information. Which one of them was in error? Or did the broad spectrum of his neuro-radionic powers merely include the ability to teleport himself out of trouble, while other, less unique individuals were limited to teleportation alone? If so, what other latent powers slumbered within him, awaiting the required stimuli to arouse them to usefulness?

It was certainly an intriguing thought to play with!

Just then he glimpsed a sparkle of silver light from the corner of his eye. Craning around, he searched the skies about him. His nerves tightened with a thrill of shock as he saw, about a half-mile behind his plane, and two thousand feet above it, several small, bright, oddly shaped flying objects. He could not make them out in any detail, such was the distance, but they were too small to be planes or helicopters.

He remembered that he was in the practice of keeping a powerful pair of binoculars in the briefcase, along with his collection of maps. He dug the case out, unsnapped it, and set the binoculars to his eyes.

The distant row of bright, silvery objects ballooned in size. He went cold as he saw clearly what they were: manlike in shape and size, but made all of some chrome-bright metal, or perhaps clothed in strange costumes of silvery foil.

There were (he now saw) seven of them in all, strung out across the sky like Christmas-tree lights. They flew in an odd position, heads pointed up at the sky, arms straight down at their sides, legs dangling limply; it was as if they were man-sized silvery puppets, suspended on invisible wires. He stared at them, perspiration beading his forehead, feeling the uneasy fringes of cold fear brush his heart.

What on earth held them up—made them fly? He saw no blur of propellers, no jet backpack, no mechanism of any kind that could account for their uncanny levitation.

Were they men in tight-fitting silver suits, or some kind of robots? It was impossible to say, but one thing about them was disturbingly inhuman. *They had no faces!*

If they were men, their faces were covered with blank, oval masks of silvery metal!

They were flying above the earth in ever-broadening circles. Tracing that circle to its center, Lux stiffened as he realized the aerial search must have started from the house where he had just spent the night —the house of his old friend, Dr. Jonas Havering!

Expressionless faces inhumanly blank, dangling stiffly like jointed wooden puppets, the seven Silver Men flashed swiftly in ever-widening circles through the bright sunlight. There was something cold and menacing in the fixity of their purpose, something ominous in their rapid, swooping flight: they were like men—hunting!

And they were hunting—*him.*

John Lux felt a moment of stark terror. The fantastic flying figures of glinting silver had not as yet noticed or bothered to investigate his small plane. But he knew it would not be very long before the broadening circles of their flight brought his craft into the area of their scrutiny.

It occurred to him then that perhaps he could escape them through his powers of teleportation. The Lady Lis had called him a neuro-radionic superman, and had told him that in moments of extreme danger his mind somehow reached out to adjust the energy flowing through the nearest power source, enabling him to bend space, teleporting himself to safety.

Well . . . actually she had not exactly used the word "teleportation" in connection with his neuro-radionic abilities, but the inference was an obvious one. Teleportation must require an enormous expenditure of energy, and the energy had to come from somewhere.

Now's the time, Lux thought, *to try a bit of teleportation!* He was certainly in danger, and Lis had called the Silver Men deadly killers. He gathered his will and tried to visualize a street corner in Weston he had visited earlier in the year. Concentrating all of his mind on that mental image, Lux sought to focus his will with all of his strength.

A few moments later he gave it up and relaxed. Nothing at all had happened!

He looked about him through the transparent cabin. In the brief time he had consumed in his vain efforts to exercise his teleportational powers, the flying silver figures had come much closer. The interval between them and his plane was narrowing rapidly. They were arrowing swiftly through the sky in his direction. The skin at the nape of his neck prickled uneasily as he sensed an ominous purposefulness in the silent, deadly speed with which the foremost of the seven magically suspended figures hurtled toward his plane.

Lux had been flying at about three thousand feet. Now he glanced down at the landscape below: green plains and rolling hills, the flash and glitter of small lakes among wooded hills, here and there a small, neat farm, gray concrete highways criss-crossing the landscape, vanishing away to the horizons. Up ahead a rather sizable stand of forest was visible, leaves brown and gold with the first few frosts of autumn. The wood covered perhaps fifty or sixty acres, and a few miles beyond it lay the outskirts of Weston.

He kicked the plane over and started down in a long, steep glide.

Glancing back, he saw the seven bright figures were darting after him in rapid pursuit. He wondered grimly how long they would continue on his trail. Would they risk being seen, for example? If he were somehow to manage to elude them and reach the Weston airfield, would they vanish? Or close with him to destroy the plane?

With growing desperation, Lux realized he did not yet know the rules of the dangerous game he was playing. Perhaps Malaire would call off his dogs, rather than have them sighted by observers—but probably not. Most likely, it would be a matter of complete indifference to the sinister master of Arthex if the activities of his agents were discovered by the authorities. What possible harm could they do to him, since he dwelled in the remote future, two hundred thousand years distant?

He was flying quite low now, virtually hedge-hopping, but there was no farm here in the proximity of the dense woods ahead. For a brief moment Lux considered landing on the highway and flagging down a passing car. But what good would that do? The Silver Men would kill him, and it could hardly matter to them if they had to destroy a car or two, and a handful of innocent motorists as well, so long as they killed John Lux!

They were all around him now, expressionless, masklike faces peering at him through the transparent cabin. One had pulled ahead and was flying alongside the engine. As Lux watched, the being leveled his metallic arm, pointing directly at the engine. A dart of incredibly brilliant blue-white flame speared out!

Lux choked back on the stick instinctively. The motor coughed and died. The plane stalled, and fell swiftly. Air shrieked as the knife-sharp leading edges of his wings tore through it. Green meadows swung dizzily up toward him in a blur of motion. Unfreezing his hands from their deathlike grip on the stick, Lux flailed out desperately, switching the ailerons.

The plane came out of her dive reluctantly; as her nose came up and the undersurface of her wings caught the force of the wind, her fall slowed. Fighting the controls with frenzied strength, he brought the dead plane down to a bumpy landing in the meadow. The rolling ground sped by underneath the bouncing wheels. The plane jolted along bone-shaking, tooth-rattling violence. The dark wall of trees swept up toward him swiftly; for one terrible moment, Lux feared the plane would plow straight into the edge of the woods, but it came to a halt only a dozen yards from the first of the trees.

Lux threw open the cabin door and half fell, half climbed out, dropping to the thick grass. His heart was hammering against his ribs and his knees felt weak and wobbly, but he was unharmed. He glanced up and saw the Silver Men sinking down toward him.

Without a moment's thought he turned and made for the woods in a staggering run. In a second or two he was among the trees. He kept going straight in as darkness closed around him. Twigs whipped his face, plucked and tore at the sleeves of his suit jacket. He stumbled over tangled roots, crashed through thick bushes, blundered into tree trunks. But he made all possible speed and got as far into the forest as he could.

After about twenty minutes of this, he came to a halt in a small glade and paused to catch his breath, listening. Had they followed him into the woods? He could hear nothing except the twittering of birds, the rustle of wind in the leaves. If the Silver Men had followed him into the forest, surely he would be able to hear them as they pushed through rustling bushes, dry branches snapping like pistol shots. But he heard nothing. Had he eluded them after all?

Then a flash of silver caught his eye. Glancing up, startled, he saw a silver figure drifting above the treetops some distance away. Its blank, masklike visage was bent, as if searching the forest beneath it.

Icy panic slammed through him! He flung himself out of sight, desperately, and rolled under a thick clump of bushes. The grass was damp here, and covered with the mulch of decaying leaves, but Lux plowed deeper under the thick-leafed branches, heedless of the wet filth.

He lay there for a long time without moving, listening intently. But all was still.

After a long time, still shaken by the closeness of his escape, exhausted by his exertions, he might have dozed for a bit.

It was the glow of strange orange light that snapped him out of his doze. Surely that ruddy light could not be sunset—it must be noon, at the latest!

He crawled out from under the bushes and gingerly ventured out into the clearing, looking around warily. He could see no sign of the Silver Men. But to the south, brilliant gold and orange light shone fiercely and waveringly.

The forest was afire!

Unable to spot him through the thick brush, the Silver Men obviously thought to flush him out into the open. They must have ignited the edge of the woods much in the same way their leader had blasted the engine of his airplane.

He looked around, despairingly. The foliage was crisping in an early fall, and as there had been no rain to speak of in several weeks, the woods were dry as tinder. Although the wind was blowing in his direction, he could smell no smoke as yet, but from the furious bright gold he knew that a tremendous conflagration was raging through the woods, and the wind was bringing it straight for him.

There was no real alternative: he must get out of the forest or be burned alive!

He plunged off into the woods again, at random. The red brilliance grew brighter and brighter, and it might have been only his imagination, but Lux thought he could almost feel the searing heat beating around him. He crashed through the woods and eventually emerged, panting, face scratched, suit besmirched with muck, to stand staring about him.

None of the Silver Men was visible at the moment. But then, a wood this size would be difficult to survey. They must be floating about up there somewhere, circling, scrutinizing the perimeter of the wood in their flight. With a bit of luck he might be away from here before one of them saw him.

The highway to Weston lay in front of him, beyond a long, sloping meadow. He made for it and began flagging cars. There were few of them at this hour, and the ones that did come by continued on without stopping. Lux realized he must have looked quite menacing, a tousled, muddy, wild-eyed figure, lurching along breathlessly, windmilling his arms. No wonder the cars speeded up, zipping by without stopping. If he had been driving one of them, he would doubtless have done the same.

Eventually, a battered pickup truck slowed to let him aboard. The driver was a garrulous farmer of fifty or so, heavy-set, grizzled, good-humored. As Lux slumped exhaustedly in the seat beside him, the old farmer cocked a mild eye at him and made some sympathetic remark about how it must be hard to hitch a ride these days, folks not being so friendly as they used to be. Then the talkative fellow embarked on a long, rambling anecdote about his younger days, when he had "rode th' rails" from Baltimore to Sacramento, stopping off to pick tomatoes for truck farmers when his cash got low. Lux grinned wearily, realizing that the garrulous farmer had mistaken him for a hobo.

He got off on the outskirts of Weston, deciding against giving the friendly old fellow a five-dollar tip. Let the farmer continue thinking he had helped a fellow knight of the road in distress; it would only disillusion him to learn the hitchhiker was a millionaire several times over.

The friendly farmer waved a cheerful good-bye and rattled off in the old truck. Lux looked around; this section of the city ran to red-brick warehouses, crumbling tenements, railroad yards. A gnawing emptiness in his middle reminded Lux that he had eaten nothing since the superb dinner Havering had served last night. He spotted a Pullman diner down the block a ways, and headed for it.

While the red-haired, gum-chewing waitress instructed the cook that Lux wanted his double order of scrambled eggs nice and dry, his triple order of bacon done crisp, and started setting out a plate for him, Lux retired to the men's room and began renovating his appearance. Crawling through the woods had turned his expensive, hand-tailored suit into a baggy, filthy, creased mess. With wadded paper towels and hot water, Lux cleaned off the worst of the filth. He washed his face and hands, combed his hair, and returned to his meal in a fairly presentable condition.

There were a number of seedy, rundown residence hotels in this part of town. Lux chose the one that looked the cleanest and took a room under an assumed name. The bored clerk looked up from his racing form just long enough to notice that Lux had no luggage, and asked for thirty dollars in advance.

The room was not so bad, considering. The radiator clanked dismally, releasing random jets of steam; the dripping faucet in the sink had left a huge rust spot; the carpet was worn and faded to the point at which its original color and pattern were undiscoverable. But the bed looked comfortable enough, and Lux thought he could endure the place for a day or two, at least.

Tomorrow he should find a store and buy fresh underlinen, socks, and maybe a new shirt, if his funds could be stretched that far. On second thought, he decided, upon examining the low state of the exchequer, to visit his bank before making any purchases. He took off his suit, stretched out on the bed, and slept for a few hours, waking at six o'clock in the evening.

He dressed, and, noting his bestubbled jaw, mentally added shaving equipment to his list of purchases. Locking the door behind him, he strolled out, not drawing even an indifferent glance from the desk clerk, found a bar and grill around the corner, and dined frugally. Stopping by the corner newsstand on the way back to his hotel, he bought a pack of cigarettes and glanced idly over the newspapers—and his blood froze in his veins as he saw *his own picture* staring up at him, under a headline that screamed

SEEK MILLIONAIRE IN HAVERING MURDER

With shaking hands, Lux snatched up a copy of the paper, dropped a dime in front of the blind news vendor, and bundled the paper under his arms. Once safely back in his room, he unfolded that paper and read the complete news story with a mixture of amazement and horror.

Sept. 1 (UP) Midhampton District Attorney James Mitchell O'Leary told reporters this morning that prominent industrial magnate John Lux, of this city, was believed to be the last person to see retired Brix College educator Jonas T. Havering alive.

Lux, millionaire head of Lux International Industries, paid an unannounced early evening visit to the Havering home in Forest Gardens, dined with the murder victim, and presumably spent the night as his guest, according to the testimony supplied by the late Prof. Havering's man servant, Louis Komo, who discovered his employer dead in his bed, reportedly of strangulation, early this morning. Komo, who called Sheriff Omar J. Peabody to report the death, also reported that Lux had left the house unobserved sometime during the night.

No motive for the apparently senseless crime has yet been discussed. Havering, a former professor in the psychology department of Brix College in Wingate Falls, was 67 years old, unmarried, and lived quietly. Author of several textbooks in his chosen field. . .

Lux skipped down the column hurriedly, looking for the next appearance of his name.

In response to queries from reporters, Mr. O'Leary said that the present whereabouts of John Lux are not known. He has not been seen either at his fashionable East Side town house in the upper 60s or at his extensive country estate on Lake Macnamara, and is believed to have fled the city, although, according to District Attorney O'Leary, "several leads on the whereabouts of the industrialist, who is wanted for questioning but has not yet been formally charged with any criminal act, have turned up, and it is only a matter of hours . . ."

He threw down the paper and sat back dumbly, shaken to the core of his being. The horror he felt at the death of his friend was shock enough, but to discover that the police were searching for him in connection with the murder unnerved him to the point of numbness. His first impulse was to pick up the phone and contact the prominent law firm he retained to handle both business problems and his personal affairs. But to do that, he reflected, would be to expose his hiding place to common knowledge.

The mysterious woman who had appeared in his

bedroom in the early hours of the morning had warned that the next twenty-four hours were crucial. She had said—wrinkling his brow, Lux strove to recall her exact words—"I advise you not to return to the city. Go to another city where you are not so well known—take rooms under an assumed identity—lose yourself in the crowd. And keep hidden—at all costs you must survive the next twenty-four hours!"

At all costs, you must survive the next twenty-four hours . . . Lux realized she had not expanded on this admonition, nor stated her reasons. The assumption was obvious: after that time it would be unlikely for some reason, that Malaire would continue his attempts on the life of John Lux. The Lady Lis had made this statement at approximately six o'clock in the morning. Glancing at his watch, Lux saw that it was now fifteen minute past eight in the evening.

In exactly ten hours, if Lis was correct, he would be safe.

He resolved to remain in hiding here until that time, and as soon as the crisis period ended to contact his lawyers. It suddenly struck him that her prediction might well be inaccurate; suppose Malaire was still seeking his life? Lux would call his lawyers and they would advise him to give himself up to the local police. The papers and wire services would get wind of the fact that he had been taken into custody in Weston, and Malaire would soon know his precise whereabouts. If the Lady Lis was *not* correct in saying he would be out of danger by tomorrow morning, he might well be murdered in his cell by an invisible hand—or by the Silver Men.

Lux felt a surge of irritation; he was immobilized, helpless to know what to do and not to do, because he was not in possession of all the facts. Why was the young woman so certain he would be in no further danger by tomorrow morning? How could she be so sure?

To these questions, as to many others, Lux had no answers at all. In the absence of evidence to the contrary, he must assume that the Lady Lis had advised him correctly.

Stretching out on the bed, Lux began putting facts together. Obviously, he had done the right thing, quitting the Havering house immediately and flying out of town. He recalled that when he had first seen the Silver Men they had been searching a wide area, branching out from the house of Dr. Havering. It seemed likely that Malaire had traced him to Havering's home. Not finding him there, the Silver Men had perhaps awakened and interrogated Havering learning all they could, they had slain him and begun the search. They had forced Lux's plane down, and were perhaps somewhere in the vicinity, aware that he had probably found a hiding place in the nearby city of Weston.

By the time the morning newspapers hit the streets, if the Silver Men were still in operation and still remained in the vicinity of Weston, they would know exactly where to find him. The key question was—*would it be safe to turn himself in, or was Lis in error?*

Tightening his jaw grimly, Lux realized he had no alternative but to let himself be taken into custody. His money was running out, and he could hardly turn up at the bank to withdraw more without being arrested as soon as the bankers realized who he was.

He understood, of course, what these terrible events added up to.

Malaire was trying to force him out into the open.

Perhaps the mysterious master of the Living City did not dare search all of Weston for him. Perhaps he did not dare risk exposing the Silver Men to discovery while they sought out the hiding place of John Lux. So Jonas Havering had to die, to seal the doom of the neuro radionic superman; to force him into further flight, or to force him into the custody of the police, and into the clutches of the electric chair.

For this, the callous master of the future had murdered an innocent man, had destroyed a brilliant, scholarly intelligence, had killed his friend.

Lux forced grief from his mind, thinking grimly of revenge. ·

IV. *The Death Trap*

JOHN LUX woke the next morning tense, irritable, and in a vile mood. He had slept poorly, tossing and turning, his dreams a jumble of harrowing hair's-breadth escapes from silent, menacing, shadowy figures. Fumbling with the watch on the bedside table, he saw it was seven A.M. Presumably, he was now safe and could contact his lawyers without fear of giving himself away to the forces that sought his death.

He washed, conscious of a day's growth of beard and the lack of clean linen, and left the hotel in search of a place to eat. It was a gray, overcast day, and the air was raw. On his way to the bar and grill, he found a small drugstore and purchased a razor, shaving cream, a toothbrush, and a tube of toothpaste. He devoured the badly cooked breakfast with gusto, for all his tension and ill humor. Paying the bill, he got change from the cashier and placed a call to the home of his lawyer, in a fashionable suburb of Midhampton.

The tinny voice shrilled incredulously: "John, is that *you?* What in the world have you done?"

"I've done nothing," Lux responded curtly. "I spent the night at the house of an old friend, and took a hotel room the next day—"

"*Nothing?* Do you realize they have a four-state alarm out for you, with orders to shoot you on sight?"

Lux felt stunned. After a moment, he said: "But why? Oh, I know I'm wanted as a material witness, because I was in the house at the time, but I had nothing to do with Havering's death, and the police are bound to realize they have no case against me. There's no conceivable motive . . ."

The lawyer's voice shook with fury. "Are you mad—as they are saying on the radio? Don't you know you left fingerprints all over the murder room? On the doorknob—on the lenses of the broken spectacles that were found beside the body—even on the—"

Lux gasped. "I was never even *in* the Doctor's bedroom—I don't even know what room he sleeps in! Why should they accuse me of wanting to kill one of my oldest friends why, the very idea is crazy—"

"That's just it! Havering kept case notes—didn't you know? They found a file with your name on it, dated the night of your visit. You came rushing in, according to Havering's account, babbled some insane tale of being pursued by invisible forces, went into a fury when he suggested psychiatric treatment, drank yourself into a stupor at the dinner table, and behaved in general like a maniac."

"But—but this is all crazy! It wasn't like that at all!" Lux protested feebly.

"They've got testimony from your secretary, who says you fired a pistol at some invisible enemy in your office the day before yesterday. Your chauffeur says you thrust him out of the car and drove off in an agitated state, as if something was chasing you. A fellow at the airport says you turned up the next morning, only an hour after Havering was killed, in terrible shape—white as paper, shaking like a leaf, babbling and muttering to yourself—hid your car in the back of a hangar, and flew off, after trying to bribe him to keep his mouth shut and say you hadn't even been there!"

"But I wasn't—I didn't—"

"The police found your plane abandoned in a field outside of Weston, after complaints that you had been buzzing the cars on the highway and a farmhouse or two—John, the police are calling you a homicidal maniac, and they mean to shoot you on sight!—John? Are you still th—"

Lux hung up, hands trembling with emotion, and sat there in the stuffy booth for a long time before stumbling out.

Back in his room, having bought some sandwiches and two large containers of coffee from the restaurant, Lux locked the door and sat down on the bed, feeling depleted.

He could not believe that Havering's reputed notes on his teleportation experiences were authentic. Havering had listened sympathetically, had discussed the phenomena intelligently, had never even suggested psychiatric treatment. Why, they had even discussed and discarded the theory of possible mental derangement—Havering himself had dismissed the notion firmly!

The only conclusion Lux could reach was that the notes were false—fake evidence, somehow planted by his unseen adversaries. But what about the fingerprints, and the distorted evidence given by his secretary, the mechanic at the airport, and—presumably—by motorists and farmers?

It would seem that Malaire's powers extended to other things beside manipulating automobiles and automatic pistols with invisible forces. It would seem he could manipulate minds as well.

Obviously, to give himself up to the police would not be the wisest thing. The evidence accumulating against him added up to a devastating total.

His only ace in the hole was his own neuro-radionic power. How this could help him out of his dilemma had yet to be seen, but the power should certainly come in handy if he had to run for his life. On a sudden impulse, Lux decided to experiment with it a little.

A small chair and table stood in the corner, with a lamp upon the table, Lux removed the shade, switched the lamp on, and unscrewed the bulb.

There before him lay an exposed and energized power source.

He drew the chair up to the table, seating himself

on it, and fixed his gaze upon the empty socket. Then, concentrating intently, he tried to reach out and tap the energy consciously. He strove to focus his mind—to *extend* himself—to soak up the energy flow.

After twenty minutes he abandoned the experiment as futile, with nothing more than a slight headache for his efforts. As yet, he could not exercise his mutant abilities consciously. Sitting back, he drank some coffee and smoked a couple of cigarettes, relaxing. What was it that the Lady Lis had said? He strove to recall her exact words—

Your ability to manipulate energies is still in its instinctual phase, and you do not yet know how to control it.

Instinctual. Let's see: thus far, he had been able to use his powers only when his life was endangered, when he was in momentary danger of being destroyed. Lux wondered if his dormant powers somehow could be linked up with the survival mechanism of his brain.

He remembered one of Dr. Havering's lectures on this mysterious brain center, back in college. The existence of the survival mechanism was debatable—was highly questionable—but certain evidence existed to suggest the presence in the human brain of a "higher authority" than mere reasoning. To support this contention, Havering had called attention to the action of a person whose hand accidentally touches a hot stove. The hand is snatched away almost instantaneously. Timed reaction tests had demonstrated that people who unknowingly touched a hot stove snatched their hands away faster by microseconds than was theoretically possible. It consumes a measurable amount of time to move your hand away from something; psychologists have traced the process from the consciousness center, where the desire to move the hand originates, through the nerve channels, by which the coded command impulse travels to the portion of the brain controlling the motor nerves, and thence to the muscles themselves, which must contract in order to move the hand. Nerve impulses move at a specific rate, and the complete process, from first idea to finished act, consumes a measurable interval of time.

But in an emergency, it seems, some "higher authority" takes over, shortcutting the complicated process, and *directly* "commands" the hand to move. No conscious volition has been observed. Hence, some psychologists have theorized that an emergency brain center exists which can perform complicated body activity sequences in virtually no time at all. This survival mechanism, they posit, is the mysterous seat of the instincts.

Lux knew, as most informed persons know, that large areas of the brain have no known use. Yet they are there, alive, supplied with blood, presumably functioning, or at least functional at need. Havering had suggested as a possible site for this survival center a prominent segment of the brain called the supra-converse lobe—although this was purest conjecture. He discussed this particular segment of the brain as a possible site because anatomical research had demonstrated that the lobe contains an extraordinarily high number of nerve connections, and the use or purpose of this part of the brain remains completely unknown.

It seemed likely, as Lux considered the matter, that his ability to teleport must be in some way connected to the survival mechanism or center, as use of the ability was certainly a high survival factor. The problem was to learn how to exert conscious control over the ability. This *might* be possible, although he reminded himself that a very large number of the body's activities were *not* under the control of the conscious mind and never could be, such as the heartbeat, the action of the glandular ducts, the digestive process, and so on.

Using a sheet of yellowing notepaper with the hotel's letterhead he found tucked inside the top drawer of the battered desk beside the bureau, he sketched out what little data he had thus far worked out. The list was disappointingly lacking in details:

1. When in bodily danger, survival mechanism triggers teleport skill.
2. Teleport "organ" taps energy flow from nearest available power source.
3. Organ bends space, or something, instantaneously moving body to safe location out of danger.

Fumbling in his trousers pocket, Lux drew out an old-fashioned penknife, a relic of his grandfather, which he always carried for sentimental reasons. Then he screwed the lightbulb back into its socket, thinking that when his teleport organ tapped the lamp's power source, the bulb might dim visibly.

He lay his left hand palm-down on the table and tried to stab it. After a few tries he decided, with a touch of wry humor, that the survival mechanism had available to it less complicated ways to avoid bodily injury. For at the last moment, each time he had tried to stab his left hand his right hand, holding the knife, either flinched away or "pulled its punch." He decided he would somehow have to fool himself into not knowing when the blow would fall. Lifting his eyes to the naked bulb to observe any dimming or flickering of the light, he began—lightly—to poke the knife about the table at random. On the fourth such try he stuck the point of the knife into his hand, and stifled a yell at the burst of pain.

Cursing vividly, he got to his feet, knocking over the chair in the process, and went into the bathroom, leaking blood all the way. He had stuck himself in the fleshy part of the hand, between the forefinger and the middle finger, a fraction of an inch beyond the knuckles. It hurt abominably, and as he washed the cut with soap and hot water, and used wadded tissues as an improvised bandage, he wished he had thought to sterilize the knife blade in a match flame before trying to sink it into his flesh.

He had learned a little from the crude experiment—not very much, but something at least. *The survival mechanism somehow knows when the im-*

pending bodily damage is negligible.

That meant he was going to have to devise . . . a death trap.

During the next half-hour or so he considered six or seven ways of killing himself, but decided against most of them. He could throw himself out of the window of this fifth-floor room, but that might attract attention. He could stick his finger into a light socket, but he doubted if that would supply a killing amount of voltage. It might simply give him one hell of a shock, which was nothing to look forward to.

The least attention-getting and probably most murderous trick was the one upon which he eventually settled. He would securely knot his silk tie around the frame that held up the shower curtain, tie the other end around his throat, and, standing on the edge of the bathtub, throw himself forward into space. Just in case the wary survival mechanism chose an easy way out again, he decided to tie his wrists together behind his back with his handkerchief. This proved a bit of a problem until he realized he could tie them together in front of his chest, holding the end of the handkerchief in his teeth to tighten the knot, and then, stooping over, put his feet through and straighten up with his hands behind his back.

It turned out to be much more difficult than it sounded, and it took a number of false tries, but at last he stood teetering on the edge of the high, old-fashionable bathtub, his tie knotted with uncomfortable tightness around his throat.

He felt extremely foolish. And it took considerable will power to hurl himself forward into space, knowing that he could either break his neck or die painfully of strangulation if he did not teleport. And just suppose that what the Lady Lis had really meant by saying in twenty-four hours he would no longer be in any danger from Malaire was that after twenty-four hours his ability to teleport would *desert him?*

John Lux resolved to find out.

Gritting his teeth, he threw himself into the air. A

band of solid iron contracted around his neck with crushing, agonizing force that sent yellow pain lancing through his mind, and—

—he found himself lying face down on the bed, twenty feet away!

Untying himself with no little difficulty, Lux examined his neck in the bathroom mirror. It was red and bruised and swollen and very tender; he soaked a towel in water from the cold tap and held it against his reddened flesh.

The tie still hung from the shower-curtain frame. A loop the size of his throat was still knotted in it. A peculiar chill ran down Lux's spine as he realized what he had discovered.

He had *dematerialized* himself!

As a dematerialized cloud of atomic particles, he had projected himself across the room!

By this time it was early evening. He had worked at his experiments all day, and had long since consumed his supply of coffee and sandwiches. A yawning void in his middle convinced him it was time to knock off for supper. It had been a gray, overcast morning and a cloudy day, and as he left the hotel it was raining ever so slightly. Around the corner from the hotel entrance, he chanced to look up, and was struck through with ice-cold shock to see—

The Silver Men!

There were only two of the weird, puppetlike, faceless monstrosities visible. They hovered only a few yards above the tops of the buildings, and from their slow, methodical movements Lux realized with a thrill of alarm that they were scrutinizing the area, using subtle senses he could not name. They would float above each building in turn, motionless for long moments, as if telepathically exploring every room in the structure, and then they would float on to the next.

Without stopping to think, Lux darted around the corner, raced across the street against the traffic, and darted down the next street, frantic to put as much distance between himself and the grim, faceless adversaries who hunted him so remorselessly as he possibly could.

Sprinting madly through the rain-swept street, Lux realized he was giving way to panic. Worse, he was attracting attention to himself, for passers-by, in raincoats or protected by umbrellas, turned to watch him with curiosity as he skidded past them.

Not only that, but on foot he could hardly hope to outdistance the Silver Men. He needed a swifter mode of transportation. The Greyhound bus terminal, he realized, was a few blocks away; he made for it as fast as possible.

A moment later a cab pulled up smoothly to the curb just ahead of him. Leaving the motor running and the door open, the driver got out and ambled over to an all-night coffee bar. Without a moment's hesitation, without even stopping to analyze the wisdom or the folly of the action, Lux slid into the driver's seat, slammed the door, and gunned the cab into the street. Behind him an astonished yell of outrage sounded, and he glanced in the rearview mirror to see the cabdriver at the curb, waving a clenched fist and shouting after him. He drove on; the only thought in his mind at the moment was to put as much distance between him and the hunters as he could.

Five minutes later he was beyond city limits, hurtling along a rainy highway. A passing sign informed him that he was on Riverside Highway, which, following the course of the Saskatonic, curved in a half-circle for several miles, keeping the city of Weston as the hub of that circle. He spat a curse between clenched teeth, realizing he was not getting any farther from the city—and the Silver Men!

A sign came whipping past him; it was blurred in the rain, but he could read it:

BRIDGE TURNOFF—500 YDS.

That was just the thing, he thought! He could see nothing behind him in the rearview mirror, or even by craning his head out of the window and looking back. Had the Silver Men started after him in pursuit, or were they still searching the city block by block, building by building, with cold, merciless efficiency? There was no way to tell.

A gust of rain caught him in the face, almost blinding him. Suddenly, he saw that he was almost past the turnoff. He slammed the steering wheel around desperately, skidding on two wheels, then went wobbling onto the bridge that crossed the river. But he was going too fast and wobbling too much. His wheels slid in a puddle of rainwater, the car whipped around in a crazy zigzag and crashed through the railing with a bone-jarring crunch.

A sheet of gray, rain-pocked water swung up before him—the cab shuddered to the shattering impact, as thousands of tons of solid water came up to smash against the windshield—and in the next instant, Lux was fighting for his life in a sinking car.

A deluge of ice-cold water squirted through the half-open window. In an instant the car was awash, and settling fast. Roiling water slid up past the windows and darkness closed in. Somehow, Lux could not get out from under the wheel—could not get the door open. The car was filling rapidly—water was up to his chest—to his face—

Should you be trapped, and find yourself in a completely hopeless situation . . . hold the tube to your ear. It will guide you to a place of safety . . .

Those last words the Lady Lis had spoken to him came into his mind suddenly as he wrestled with the jammed door in the rapidly filling car. He clawed the tube out of his inside breast pocket and pressed it against his ear.

A burst of high-speed chatter, like static, sounded tinnily.

And—*nothing happened!*

The water closed over his face. He fought on in the cold darkness, but with a growing sense of futility. The door would not open—and even if it did, John Lux had never learned how to swim.

The metal tube was his last resort . . . and it had failed.

Why couldn't he teleport? He tried to, desperately, but with no result.

He could hold his breath no longer; his lungs were on fire, and his brain felt as if it were about to explode.

Teleport, damn you, tele—

Then his resolve gave way; his will crumpled.

His jaws had been clamped shut against the flood, so tightly that the muscles of his cheeks stood out like iron bands. Now, slowly, reluctantly, he pried his jaws open. Frantic for air, his starved lungs taut-stretched drums filled with pain, John Lux opened his mouth.

Gagging, choking, he swallowed the cold, filthy water of the polluted river. And darkness whirled up around him; water closed about him in a giant, crushing hand. The consciousness of death fell about his brain like fingers of black ice. They closed, crushing out the last spark of consciousness . . .

But to the extinction of that last, flickering thought, his will fought on:

Teleport! Teleport! TELE—"

Then the world ended for John Lux, and he knew no more.

V. *The Null Sphere*

JOHN LUX lay there for a long time, weak and groggy. He had vomited up all the river water he had swallowed, in painful, racking spasms that left him exhausted. Eventually he dragged himself to his feet and looked around, bemusedly.

The ground around him was composed of low, rolling hummocks that only the most charitable could describe as hills. The soil was dry and parched, breaking, here and there, into low brush like gorse or heather. The sky was leaden and colorless, reflecting his own drained, enervated mood.

He was soaked to the skin, his suit was a sodden mess, and he was cold and miserable. Hungry, too; hungrier than he had been upon leaving the hotel. The rain seemed to have stopped, and the sun lay low in the west—at least, he assumed it must be the west. It was a pale, dull sun, warmthless and ruddy.

Looking around at the bleak landscape, he wondered how far he had teleported this time. The river was nowhere in sight. For lack of a better idea, he picked out the tallest hummock in sight and trudged towards it, thinking to get his bearings from the view of the surrounding countryside the crest would afford.

If he had not been so weak and exhausted and dull-witted, he might have singled out the several curiosities of the landscape much earlier. As it was, though, it was not until he had climbed up the heather-grown hill to its top and stared about that some of the strangeness dawned on his consciousness.

For one thing, it had been pouring rain when his

stolen car went out of control, plunging into the river. Now, not only was it not raining, but from the dry, crumbling condition of the soil, it could not have rained here in days. Had he been unconscious after teleporting out of the sinking car? *Could* he have lain unconscious long enough for the ground to dry so thoroughly?

For another thing, this landscape did not in the least resemble the countryside around Weston. That land had been all green meadows, neat farms, wooded hills. But *this* bleak and barren landscape, all low hummocks, patchily grown with rough low brush, purple and gold, like heather, looked more like sub-Arctic tundra or the Russian steppes, or even the lowlands of Scotland!

How far *had* he teleported this time?

From the low eminence of the hilltop he could not see the slightest sign or token of human habitation. If Weston itself was too far away to be visible, surely he should have spotted the familiar haze of pollution that hangs over most industrial cities. But he saw no sign of civilization at all. No highways cut across the limitless rolling plain; no farms spread out the checkerboard pattern of their plowed fields; there were not even any planes visible aloft. *Nothing.*

It was then that he began to pay attention to that peculiar sun.

He had left the hotel in early evening. *But this sun was coming up!*

Could he have lain unconscious all night long? He supposed it was possible, although hardly probable; but it seemed the only explanation that would fit the observable facts.

At any rate, he had eluded his pursuers. He was shivering with cold in his sodden garments, and hunger gnawed viciously at his empty stomach, but he was still alive, at least. Now he needed food and warmth and shelter.

Picking a direction at random, he began trudging off in the direction of the sunrise. After the first hour he felt somewhat better; the exercise, and the sunshine, pale as it was, had dried his clothing for the most part, and had warmed him through and through. He was still famished, though, and regarded the desolate landscape around him with growing unease—with growing consciousness that something was very wrong. This kind of land ought not to be found anywhere within a thousand miles of Weston and Midhampton, and in such a heavily populated, urbanized, industrial state, he ought not to be able to walk for an hour without seeing *some* signs of civilization. He still had not even seen a plane—or a single tree, for that matter.

Again, with growing unease, he wondered how far he had teleported.

Toward the middle of the afternoon, Lux finally saw evidence of wildlife. In this case, it was a bird.

Or, at least, he knew no other name by which to call it. A winged flying thing ought to be a bird, by all logic and reason. He had to admit, though, that it was not particularly birdlike. And the nearer it came, and the more clearly he could see it, the less and less it looked like any kind of bird he had ever seen or heard of.

It was shaped more like a serpent or an eel than anything else. Apparently devoid of limbs—at least, if it *had* legs, he could not see them—it was all of twenty or thirty feet in length, with a blunt, wedge-shaped head. The body, though, was not really snake-like, for it had a cylindrical torso, as thick about as the pelvis of a mature man, from which the elongated neck and tail segments tapered away. From nose to tail-tip the flying thing was covered with bright-colored scales in a complicated diamond-and-stripe pattern that reminded Lux of pictures he had seen of Gila monsters.

The oddest thing about it was the wings. There were two sets of these, one at the fore end of the cylindrical torso, where the shoulders should be, and the other set at the rear. The wings flapped in synchronization, the way a dog trots. First the right forewing extended, then the left rearwing, then the left fore wing and the right rear wing; it was sort of like watching two men paddle a canoe. But there was really nothing humorous about the fantastic aerial serpent, and Lux found himself shuddering with relief once it had lazily flapped by overhead and was dwindling off to the north.

It was then that he first began to entertain suspicions that he might have teleported to the surface of another planet.

At first glance, the notion was utterly incredible. However, so was the power itself, and he began wondering, with a thrill of helpless horror, just what the mysterious future woman had meant by saying the tube would convey him to a "a safe place."

The only planet this might possibly be was Mars. This dim, bleak landscape, devoid of woods or mountains, where a faint, cool sun burned dimly in a leaden, wintry sky bore some faint resemblance to what the desert planet was supposed to be like. Some, but not much. Cursory reading of popular science articles had given him the impression that Mars was bitterly cold, and had an atmosphere so lacking in oxygen as to be gaspingly thin. And he thought Mars was supposed to have a gravity field much weaker than Earth's. If these items of information were correct, then this could not be Mars.

He kept trudging along, bearing east, for want of a better idea. The tube Lis had given him was lost somewhere—it might have fallen from his hand during teleportation; it might have rolled from his fingers as he lay there gagging up river water. At any rate, he no longer had it on his person. Again he wondered what, if anything, the tube had done. All he had been conscious of was a high-speed, high-pitched, almost inaudible gabble of sound, like a tape recorder speeded up. Had Lis tricked him—hoaxed him—lied to him? If so, why?

He had no answers to these questions, and put them away for further thought.

Hunger died from its first sharp pangs to a dull, queasy ache in his middle. When he became too weary to walk, he sat down and rested until he felt refreshed enough to rise and plod on awhile longer. The monotony of the landscape was such that after some hours of this, he simply stopped noticing it.

The pale, dull red, strangely shrunken disc of the sun crossed the sky above him and sank in what must have been the west. The humid air grew refreshingly cool. The leaden sky darkened; stars came forth upon it, but they formed no constellations with which he was familiar.

After a while the moon rose. It was larger than the moon of Earth, and its surface features bore only a superficial resemblance to that moon's familiar face. A distinct shock went through him a while later as a second moon lifted above the horizon. This one was very small, but piercingly bright, as if it had an albedo much higher than the first moon's. It was almost as brilliant as a star, but it was visibly a disc, and not self-luminous, as it was not entirely full.

The discovery that this world possessed two lunar companions heightened its resemblance to what he had heard of Mars, and he thought some more about the theory that he had teleported himself to the surface of that planet. It was an idea he could neither prove nor disprove from the slender evidence he possessed. But, an hour or so later, yet a *third* moon rose over the horizon, which made it highly unlikely that this planet was Mars. He tried to think of a planet in the solar system that had three moons, but gave up. Astronomy was a subject he had never studied, and what little he knew of the science had been picked up from casual reading.

By the time the last of the three moons was well up the sky, Lux was stumbling and numb with fatigue. He began looking around for a likely place to spend the rest of the night. It was then that he saw the Silver Men again.

They were five or ten miles behind him, strung out

across the sky, evenly spaced, moonlight flashing
from their mirror-bright silver bodies. He broke into
a stumbling, staggering run.

A dark shape became visible on the horizon to the
north, and he headed for it. He might perhaps have
been wiser to just curl up amid the heathery brush,
thus remaining unseen on the night-dark landscape.
But fatigue and hunger, a growing thirst, and a sense
of being completely lost and thoroughly helpless
goaded him into flight.

The dark mass rose up before him like a huge
rounded hill. The rolling ground leveled off as he got
nearer and nearer to the black hemisphere. He ran
on, every panting breath burning in his lungs like liq-
uid fire. When he got near enough to see the dark
mass clearly, he came to a halt and stared up at it.
He had never seen anything remotely like it in all
his life.

It must have covered several square miles, a perfect
dome of dull, completely non-reflecting black substance. It was as smooth and regular as a ball of polished obsidian. He gaped at it blankly.

Then something marvelous and weird and terrible
lifted into view from beyond its mile-high upper
arch. It was made of red metal, blood-scarlet in the
triple play of moonlight, and shaped rather like a
child's top. The bluntly rounded end of the top was
skyward, and the tapering, pointed end was toward
the ground. It was clearly an artifact, obviously the
work of intelligence, although he could imagine no
purpose for the huge hovering thing. It did not have
a smooth surface, like the colossal black sphere, but
was broken into complex aggregates of shapes:
rounded humps, tubelike protuberances, some of them
curving back into the central mass like the handles of
a pitcher or a vase, sleek bosses, oddly regular grooves
or depressions, and any number of orifices, triangular,
oval, oblong, some blackly empty and some seemingly
grilled.

He had nothing to measure the floating thing
against, but he felt certain it was immense. He got
the feeling the hovering thing was the size of several

aircraft carriers rolled into one.

The Silver Men were only a mile or two away now, but John Lux did not even think of them and the danger they represented. His mind was filled with a vast, dawning astonishment. For now he knew beyond all question what the flying mountain of red metal must be.

The Weapon Machine.

And the smooth, mile-high dome of non-reflecting darkness?

The Living City of Arthex, shielded by the Null Sphere.

And now he knew why this planet was so peculiarly familiar in its atmosphere and its gravity, but so very unfamiliar in its landscape and wildlife and moons.

For this was the world of the remote future!

He had teleported himself, not through space—but *across the gulf of time!*

And the strange wilderness world he had wandered through all that day—the weird planet, with its four-winged birdlike flying serpents and its triple moons—was his own world, his own Earth, but as it would become *two hundred thousand years* after his own age!

A number of puzzling, seemingly isolated facts suddenly fitted into a meaningful pattern.

The multiwinged snake thing, for instance, was not an example of extraterrestrial wildlife, but purely a local product. Was it what the ordinary birds, or perhaps serpents, of his own day would eventually evolve into? Perhaps; two hundred thousand years, however, sounded like far too brief an interval of time for such a drastic evolutionary change. Perhaps there had been lingering radioactive contamination in the soil or the atmosphere, left over from that sequence of future conflicts the Lady Lis had termed "the City Wars," and this radioactivity had accelerated normal evolution through sporadic mutation.

And the bewildering multiplicity of moons, too

. . . During the two thousand centuries that separated this age from his own, it would seem that the old Earth had captured two more cosmic wanderers, as it had perhaps originally captured the Moon itself.

Knowing where—or when!—he was, however, only raised a new crop of problems.

Lis had told him that the surviving remants of mankind, in its totality, dwelled within the Living City; that the world outside was an untenanted wilderness which man had abandoned to nature.

She had also told him something of the Null Sphere that covered the City like an enormous dome. She had said this curious dome of force was invulnerable to any known weapon—

Within the Null Sphere space has been artificially distorted into a kind of pseudospace wherein the laws of physics no longer apply. Neither energy nor matter can exist within the Null Sphere . . . no destructive ray or missile can penetrate it. . . . Or, to be precise, they can in fact enter it, but once they have done so they cease utterly to exist . . .

Lux felt globules of cold perspiration break out on his forehead as he recalled to memory her ominous words. In effect, then, he was marooned—helpless, unarmed and alone—in a savage, strange world empty of his own kind.

For if the unthinkably powerful armaments of the gigantic Weapon Machine had striven in vain for ten thousand years to penetrate that strange zone of black force, surely he could not get through it!

He turned, searching the dark heavens.

The Silver Men were less than a mile away, and floating towards him swiftly. Turning on his heel, he sprinted down the slope of the heather-clad depression to the very base of the enormous black dome.

It towered above him to a colossal height now. He studied the surface curiously. It looked like smooth black glass, but it was devoid of the reflecting properties of glass. It rose from the level floor of the vast, bowl-like depression in a smooth, unbroken wall of ebon darkness that curved far up above his head.

He did not quite dare to touch it with his bare hands, but, digging in one pocket of his water-stained trousers, took out one of the new copper quarters the government had recently issued, to follow the new tin pennies and aluminum nickels. Holding the coin between his fingertips by one edge, he very carefully touched the other edge of the coin against the dull dead black surface.

It sank in as if there was nothing there at all!

There was no sound or odor or flash of energy; the black wall did not oppose the entry of the copper coin in the least. He thrust the coin in until fully half of the copper disc was within the dark surface. Then he drew it out and looked at it.

Half the coin was gone! Sheared off as cleanly as could be imagined. The new edge was impossibly mirror-bright, impossibly smooth. Atom by atom, the inexplicable disruptive forces of the Null Sphere had *disintegrated* the solid copper!

Lux repressed a shiver of revulsion. If he were to plunge into that glassy-smooth zone of absolute negation, he would cease to exist in the first microsecond.

He looked around. The Silver Men were less than half a mile away, and only fifty yards above the ground. Even as he looked at them, one of the enigmatic, faceless beings leveled its arm at a hummock of dry gorse. Blue-white flame sheeted from the extended fingers; the hillock exploded into flames.

Now the other six, hovering in a broad half-circle, spewed similar gouts of blazing energy from their metallic fingers. Night vanished before the intolerable brilliance.

They were drifting closer—hedging him in!

Darts of dazzling electric fire clove smoking runnels in the dry earth. They were *herding* him—driving him back against the deadly dome of black force. Within mere seconds, he would either have to leap into the destroying zone of null force or face the spears of actinic lightning that spewed from their fingertips.

And either way meant death!

Then one lifted his silvery arm until his fingers pointed directly into Lux's eyes.

Lux tensed, hurling glances of helpless desperation from side to side, seeking a route of escape. But there was no escape—the darting rays of sparkling fire fenced him in on all sides, and his back was perilously close to the zone of black nothingness.

If only there were some place of safety to which he might teleport! But no such sheltered spot was visible; everywhere, the sparkling streams of terrific energy lanced, drawing smoking grooves in the withered soil.

The beams of electric fire flashed everywhere, purely at random. With a sense of finality, with the ring of doom behind the thought, it came to John Lux then that his still instinctive, still mindlessly cautious survival mechanism could not dare transport him anywhere on the visible landscape. For the sheer, unpredictable randomness of the darting rays precluded any single spot from offering sufficient safety!

He had escaped from difficult positions before, but from this trap there did not seem to be *any* possible escape, unless another time jump was the answer. He doubted that it was.

The beams were flashing very near him now. In just another half-second—

Then a gout of blinding energy exploded directly toward him—

VI. *The Living City*

John Lux found himself sprawling face-downward upon a slick, glassy surface.

He felt faint, drained of strength, exhausted. His limbs trembled as if from extreme fatigue. By now he was familiar with these symptoms. They were the physical reactions which always accompanied the phenomenon of teleportation.

So he *had* teleported from the place of danger! But—to where?

He lurched to his knees and came staggering to his feet. The hard, glassy stuff beneath him, he now saw, was some sort of paving material, although unlike any he had seen on an Earthly street in his own age. It was as smooth and sleek as fine porcelain, rosy white, and slightly resilient—perhaps of some spongy or elastic composition.

His eyes stung; his vision blurred; perspiration, coldly beading his brows, dribbled down into his eyes. Well, shaky or not, he had managed to elude the Silver Men one more time. Trembling with shock and exhaustion, soaked through with cold perspiration, he was still—alive!

He rubbed his eyes clear, lifted his head, and looked around him to see to what place of refuge his teleport powers had carried him this time . . . and forgot all about the pavement.

He looked on a world of wonders.

An utterly fantastic metropolis lay before him. It must have sprawled across an area of several square miles at least, and it was a bewildering maze of incredible playfulness and beauty. To every side, a throng of quaint, bizarre, fantastically colorful buildings met his gaze.

Some of the buildings were domes—complete globes, resting on slender stems, or swelling hemispheres, or faceted geodesic structures such as Buckminster Fuller designed, or throngs of teardrops and bubbles linked together.

Others were built on more complex geometric forms: cubes, prisms, parallelograms, and complicated, many-sided constructions to which he could not at once attach the proper name.

And there were towers, too: tapering spears, fluted minarets, standing slabs, soaring spires that rose to needle points, squat turrets, rounded cylinders.

Everywhere he looked, John Lux gazed upon a bewildering multiplicity of forms and shapes and sizes and gaudy, impossible hues. It took his bemused mind a few moments to make order out of the riot of colors, the variety of architectural styles.

There were towers of many tiers, vaguely reminiscent of pagodas, colored canary yellow, glistening black, and shimmering amber. There were swelling domes and bulbous globular forms that glowed or glistened with elusive, shifting tones, like titanic opals. Slim, impossibly leaning spires of brilliant gold, fierce magenta, pale silver-frost. Incredible spirals and tangled edifices of interlocked curves and angles that blazed pink and gorgeous red and virulent purple, like colossal jewels. It was the capital of Fairyland—a city transported from the Land of Oz—a dream metropolis, constructed by the Djinn!

Directly before him, a huge, square, fortress like structure loomed heavily. It was built, seemingly, of lucent blocks of pure, polished jade. Turrets crowned with peak roofs like the steeple hats worn by witches rose at each of the four corners, and the uppermost wall was notched with machicolations, like some Martian version of Camelot.

Beyond the green fortress swelled a bewildering thing composed entirely out of gleaming globes of deep sapphire, glistening argent, and frosted white.

This conglomeration of jeweled soap bubbles was topped with a forest of spear points; from each slim spire a fluttering gaudy pennant snapped in the breeze.

To the other side of the emerald fortress rose a tapering, smooth-sided pyramidlike building fashioned of immense cubes which looked as if they weighed many tons each. These cubes were alternately colored black and crimson, and the overall effect was that of a gigantic checkerboard turned into a mountain. Craning his neck, John Lux saw that a thick plume of dark green smoke spewed from its topmost level, as from a chimney. Beyond it, a slender gray and lavender tower soared like a fluted column, its crest breaking into curbing petal-shaped extrusions that curved back, exposing a ball of fiery orange.

All about him the fantastic city spread, a confusion of brilliantly colorful buildings, each different from the others, some indescribably alien, as if designed according to the tenets of some supra-Euclidian geometry with six or seven dimensions. The cityscape was a riot of unbelievable colors, an exuberance of fantastic shapes!

The richness of the hues gained depth from the fact that the sky which arched overhead was black as death, and starless. But toward the zenith of the gloomy heavens five glimmering orbs, formed in a ring perhaps a mile across, floated in a haze of light. This gyre of captive moons, or artificial suns, or whatever they were, blazed with light—brassy gold, pure yellow, faint chartreuse, milky white, and lucent silver.

Lux realized that his survival mechanism had again triggered his unique talents, teleporting him into Arthex, the Living City. And he now realized a fundamental fact concerning his ability to teleport which he had been ignorant of until now. That was that when he teleported he somehow crossed space without actually passing *through* it—for even as a disembodied cloud of atoms, he could not have penetrated to the other side of the Null Sphere without instant and total destruction.

Obviously, he had flashed out of existence in one place—and snapped into existence in another.

This might yet prove a valuable fact to know.

He had escaped, at least for the present, from the silvery and faceless enigmas who had hunted him through time and space. But he was now in an even more precarious position than before. For now he stood within the Living City itself—alone and friendless—and here his deadliest foe, the mysterious Malaire, ruled supreme.

He had penetrated the dome—not into freedom, but into the very fortress of his most implacable enemy!

Keeping to the shadows as much as possible, Lux followed the curved, meandering ways of the City, moving gradually towards its center.

Irregularity, it seemed, was the norm in Arthex.

The streets curved and wandered every which way, criss-crossing and intersecting each other like a maze, inexplicably widening to the width of an eight-lane highway, then narrowing to the breadth of an alley.

They were paved with slick, glassy porcelain—or so it looked to the eye. But the rosy-white substance was soft and resilient as rubber, and faintly warm to the touch. It reminded Lux of an experimental floor covering designed for a nursery . . .

As he approached the inner circles of the fantastic metropolis, he observed that a carnival of some sort was in progress. Faint, jangling tunes of discordant music drifted sourcelessly on the artificial breezes. A swarm of translucent globes, shimmering with wisps of color and wobbling insubstantially like enormous soap bubbles, drifted about the streets. One burst wetly against his cheek, spraying him from head to foot with dewy perfume, a delicious heliotrope.

He began to encounter hordes of people in elaborate, fantastic costumes.

An enormously fat man, with painted cheeks, scarlet lips, and blue circles painted about his eyes, danced along, leaning on a staff covered with tinkling bells. From head to foot his corpulence was draped in amazing garments of crimson and orange—flounced, puffed, beribboned, slashed, tucked, and gathered. A bell-fringed cap sat insecurely atop his round bald pate. He paid not the slightest attention to Lux.

Then a slim girl, wrapped in transparent purple gauze, her long floating tresses dyed metallic pink, her smiling face a riot of blue and yellow polka dots, came swaying by, leading on a jeweled leash a fat, funny little animal, apple green, wooly, roly-poly as a teddy bear. The comical little creature had three twinkling black eyes and waddled on eight short fat legs. The girl in purple gauze also took no notice of Lux.

Turning the next corner, Lux found himself in a throng of gaily costumed persons celebrating some sort of festival that seemed to partake equally of a Halloween masquerade, a riot, and an orgy. He stared about him, transfixed.

Two lovers, their spangled finery torn away, slender bodies gleaming nude, made passionate love on the sidewalk before him, oblivious to the throng that danced and swirled about them. Lux could not believe them any older than ten or eleven—and he could not even be certain that their underdeveloped, smoothly ambiguous bodies were of opposite sexes.

A very obese woman, tears of mirth running down her scarlet-painted face, lolled in a sort of carriage of brilliant indigo plastic, which looked as if it had been molded all in one piece. There were no wheels on the blue carriage; it floated, wobbling gently as she shifted her weight, about eleven inches above the warm, elastic pavement. The woman was drinking golden wine out of a fantastic bottle shaped like a glass flower. The pavement about her was littered with the broken remains of a half-dozen such containers. She was very, very, very drunk.

The omnipresent music swirled about, growing

louder and then fainter at random. Some of the celebrants danced together or singly; some shuffled or
swayed to the endless, tuneless rhythms. Several gaud-
ily costumed bodies sprawled about, obviously intox-
icated and unconscious. There were literally hundreds
of people of all ages in the throng that surged and
eddied through the streets.

None of the members of the throng had yet paid
the slightest attention to Lux; nevertheless, he felt
it most prudent to withdraw. He turned aside down
a narrow alley that curved like a giant S and at its
end nearly stumbled across the prone body of a
plump, soft-faced man in cream ruffles, who snored
loudly, cheek pillowed on be-ringed hands. A spangled violet cloak with attached hood was carelessly
tossed nearby. Lux snatched it up thankfully and
draped it about him, hiding his garments. Pulling the
capacious hood closely around his head, shadowing his
face, he retraced his steps.

The throng surged up and swept him into its colorful vortex. Heady clouds of warm, moist, inebriat-
ing vapors puffed about him like a drunken, varicol-
ored fog. Slim arms clasped him about the neck—a
hot, avid mouth kissed him intimately—then he was
snatched away into a ring of half-naked youths,
capering in a grotesque dance around a giggling little
man in nine shades of yellow, who played on a bejeweled instrument very much like an accordion.

He broke free—accepted a cut-glass beaker of
heavy amber fluid, shot through with sparkling bubbles but with all the fiery kick of vintage brandy,
shoved into his hand by a spectacularly naked woman
with fire-orange frizzed hair, her bare body sprayed
with beaded green glitter.

Sometime later he discovered the gustatorium. The
crowd wandered in and out in a desultory fashion,
not seeming to pay anyone for the variety of foods
and liquids they enjoyed at the small white enamel
tables of a sort of sidewalk café. Lux entered cautiously, and viewed a variety of brightly colored

foodstuffs displayed on a wall of illuminated glass boxes, not unlike a Horn & Hardart Automat. He surreptitiously observed the way other people merely pressed the stud below the box of their choice, whereupon the door flung open to one side; they took out the article and strolled off to find a table with their friends.

Lux stared at the array of foods with famished eyes. Everything looked like candy, or jello molds. He chose a variety that looked appetizing, poured himself a tumblerful of foaming black fluid, and selected a secluded corner table.

There were dainty cakes that looked like mint pastilles, pink, pale yellow, cream, and lime green. He bit into one cautiously; it dissolved in his mouth to a rich, succulent sauce like purée of asparagus. Another simulated the exact spicy aroma and chewy resilience of grilled American cheese; a third was crisp and crunchy, with the dewy freshness of chilled radish or raw cucumber. He nibbled through the stack of pastilles ravenously, gulping away at the foaming black liquor, which reminded him of an improbably delicious wedding between hot Turkish coffee and licorice.

A rounded confection that looked outwardly like a creampuff was his prime discovery. One bite and he gulped the mouth-watering succulence of a filet mignon with mushroom caps. He went back for three more of these.

An hour later he emerged from the gaily lit, crowded gustatorium deliciously replete, filled with a sense of warm well-being. But a nagging thought wormed through his mind: Why were the foods, although wholesome, delicious, and nourishing, disguised in the appearance of rich, brightly colored candies and confections?

It was almost as if they were so designed to tempt and coax spoiled children into getting a balanced diet . . .

He began to realize grimly the justice of the cause of the Arcadians. The citizens of Arthex rioted through the streets in drunken, endless play. They were indeed children, and the city itself, the fantastic toy metropolis of candy-bright colors and amusing shapes, was their eternal, self-perpetuating playground.

Yes, Lis was right! The walls of Arthex must be battered down; man must escape this brilliant, bejeweled prison. He must be coaxed or driven out into the dreary wilderness that lay beyond the black zone of force, there to learn again to fight—to struggle—and to survive. Here lay only sickness, madness, death, extinction.

From the few things the Lady Lis had told him about this portion of the Urban Age, John Lux had drawn several false conclusions.

She had depicted the Living City of Arthex as a dictatorship, its inhabitants a slave population under the tyrannical and absolute rule of the mysterious Malaire. Somehow he had envisioned a prison-like metropolis with streets filled by apathetic, dull-eyed hordes of citizenry shuffling along under the hard gaze of Gestapo-like police.

But nothing could have been further from the facts! This gay, overdecorated pleasure city with its beautifully costumed, childlike citizens romping through orgies of endless play was more like a cross between Disneyland, Coney Island, the French Riviera, and the last days of Pompeii than one of the despotic Iron Curtain slave states of his own millennium.

Nowhere did he see anything resembling police surveillance. Nor did the City present any of the obvious trappings of 1984—banners, political posters, patriotic slogans, or the like.

He became aware that the Living City itself watched over and protected its carefree denizens. Aerial contrivances like huge iridescent soap bubbles floated between the pylons and pagodas; he glimpsed many near-collisions between these aircars, and from the automatic way they bobbled apart, he deduced that robot safety monitors of some kind made it impossible for the globular vehicles to approach either the structures of the City or each other, no matter how clumsy or careless the hand on their controls.

And then there was the construction of the City itself, its resilient street paving, which prevented even the most inebriated citizen from taking injury in a fall. Ground traffic was limited to anti-gravitic sleds or sleighs, such as the one in which the very obese woman had lolled, drinking golden wine. He observed several more of these wheelless ground sleds, and noticed with what ease they automatically avoided pedestrians. When the brilliantly hued vehicles of molded plastic could progress no farther without chancing injury to the throngs that surged and eddied through the streets, he saw that they simply came to a halt, refusing to go any farther until they could continue in safety.

Everything about the City, he began to realize, was designed to protect the Arthesians from doing injury to themselves: the curving streets, the gentle inclines, the scattered buildings with their rounded edges, the lack of balconies or precipitous stairways.

The City, in fact, was a gigantic kindergarten! A kindergarten through which the people wandered aimlessly from one pleasure to the next, unobtrusively watched by the omnipresent City Brain, which remained constantly vigilant and ready to assist its beautiful and childish charges against any need.

He observed one case of this unsleeping vigilance in particular.

He had come upon a huge, bowl-shaped depression that resembled an ice-skating rink but without ice. The circular depression was ringed with little white tables under gaily colored parasols, where people in gorgeous costumes rested, sampling effervescent beverages and fruitlike snacks.

The rink was floored with some mirrorlike coating of repellent force. Citizens skidded about in laughing play, riding discs of plastic painted in bright primary colors; the discs floated a few inches above the mirrorlike pavement. Obviously, the sloping, bowl-shaped nature of the rink had been so designed as a safety factor, and accidents were rare. Nevertheless, as he paused to watch the spinning discs full of laughing carnival-goers, an accident did occur.

One of the discs spun about the outer perimeter of the bowl and curved inward sharply, to avoid collision with another. A lanky youth wrapped in floating streamers of canary-yellow gauze was flung from the disc and went crashing into one of the tables along the rim.

A crowd gathered, tittering with amusement as the youth sat there dabbling at a flesh wound on his brow, from which scarlet leaked. The boy screwed up his face and began to weep, bawling at the unaccustomed sensation of pain. The crowd laughed uproariously at his bewildered expression and tears. It did not occur to any of them to go to his assistance or to see if his injuries were anything more than merely superficial.

Observing the scene, Lux was jolted to see one of the white picnic tables come trundling over unobtrusively by itself. The white enamel table slid across the pavement on hidden wheels, and the crowd, laughing at the weeping boy, parted to make way for it as if through unconscious habit. No one but Lux seemed to pay any particular attention as the table sidled up to the red-faced boy. It extruded extensible limbs and felt the youth over carefully, then swabbed the blood from his face, smeared the scalp wound with a swift-healing gel, and popped a bright red candy into his mouth. His weeping died away in sniffles, and after a moment the boy got up and went over to a pretty girl with hair of spun chrome, her bare body covered with tinfoil polka dots in the most surprising places; he began to kiss her enthusiastically, all memory of the accident gone.

The crowd dispersed and the table returned to its original position unnoticed. Only Lux found the event remarkable.

There was no sense of passing of time in this gorgeous kindergarten-city of endless carnival.

Lux observed no clocks of any kind, and the people he passed did not seem to wear watches, although their garments came in such a vast range of design and variety of decoration that it was hard for him to be certain of this.

The five artificial suns blazed with rich and unvarying light from the center of the dead-black "sky," which was actually the undersurface of the protective Null Sphere. As hours passed, Lux observed no variation in the flood of light: in Arthex, it was always afternoon . . .

Wrapped in the spangled violet cloak, which disguised him effectively, Lux aimlessly wandered through the City.

At length he became conscious that someone was following him, keeping close on his heels.

At first he was aware only of the pressure of unseen eyes. After a while, the uneasy sensation of being deliberately followed increased.

He caught his first glimpse of the person following him in reflection. While passing a wild, glittering structure that resembled a dodecahedron whose planes were alternating mirror-bright sheets of dark indigo and brilliant silver, he noticed a man in the throng looking after him with curious intentness.

Several times thereafter, he noticed the same man in the ever-changing crowd. Since Lux was strolling about, choosing each direction at random whim, it was unlikely that he would see the same individual behind him in the crowd unless the man was actually following him.

A mood of uneasiness took possession of Lux.

A moment later he stiffened with shock as a voice spoke at his shoulder, calling him by name.

VII. *The First Arcadian*

"John Lux!"

He whirled to see who had addressed him. It was a tall, elderly man whose gaunt, unsmiling face was framed in silver locks and a silver beard. His lean body was robed in a somber gown of neutral gray, which contrasted in its simplicity of design and restraint of hue with the wildly colored, fantastical garments of the other citizens.

It was the man he had glimpsed by reflection in the mirror-paned dodecahedron building, the man whose dignity and sobriety had formed such a curious contrast to the laughing inebriated, love-making throng surging through the winding ways.

"Who are you?" Lux demanded.

"My name is Sonthus, John Lux."

"How is it that you know my name?"

The silver-haired man smiled faintly, but made no reply.

"You have been following me," Lux said. "Why? What do you want with me?"

"You need not be alarmed for your safety, John Lux," the old man remarked in a serene voice. "I am not your enemy, but your friend."

"How do you know who I am?"

Sonthus shrugged. "Your description was given to me," he said. "I would have found you sooner, but it did not occur to me that you might seek to hide your presence here behind the protective coloration of borrowed raiment." He smiled, indicating the spangled robe of violet Lux had found in the alley.

"But how did you know I would be here—my name, and how to recognize me?" Lux persisted. The other smiled gravely, and smoothed his snowy beard.

"Your description was given to me by one I might aptly term our mutual acquaintance. It was she who instructed me to be on the lookout for a stranger of your appearance."

" '*She*'—do you mean—"

Sonthus nodded sagely.

"Yes, our mutual friend—the Lady Lis."

Relief went gusting through Lux, leaving him shaken. He sagged weakly on trembling limbs and might perhaps have fallen, had not the old man gripped his arm to steady him, with strong, capable fingers which displayed surprising strength.

Lux had not been aware of the tension he had been under, alone and lost in this City of nightmarish beauty, until that tension was released, leaving him pale and trembling with reaction.

"Steady, John Lux!" his newfound friend counseled. The older man studied Lux's pale, worn face and haggard eyes with sympathy in his demeanor.

"You have endured much, I perceive. Well, now you can relax and dismiss your fears. For now you are safe—safe for a certain time, at least—and now you have a chance to rest a bit and recover yourself after your harrowing experiences. So long as I am at your side, no one will harm you or even question your presence here."

"Thanks," Lux said faintly. "It has been tough going for a while; a friend in need, and all that!"

"Do you require nutriment?" Sonthus asked. "A public gustatorium is nearby—"

Lux shook his head gratefully.

"I found one on my own, thanks; but I would really enjoy a bath and a few hours' sleep."

Sonthus nodded sympathetically.

"Of course! You must be exhausted from your exertions, and unnerved by the strangeness of your new surroundings. Come; my place of residence is not far. Lean on my arm, and let me guide you . . ."

As they went through the ever-lighted, ever-crowded streets, Lux and his new friend exchanged information. Lux wanted to know how the other had recognized him, singling him out of the busy throng.

"By your height, chiefly," Sonthus smiled. "You are taller and of much more stalwart physique than are the puny, pampered children of this decadent epoch. The Lady Lis apprised me of your coming and furnished me with your description; I have been roaming the City for hours, searching for you."

"How is it that you know her?"

Sonthus regarded him gravely.

"I am one of her remote ancestors," he remarked calmly; "she is by way of being a distant descendant of mine. Perhaps I should explain, John Lux, that I am the First Arcadian; virtually alone of the pitiful and degenerate Arthesians of this vile age, I am cognizant of the inherent dangers the protectiveness of the Living City has in its effects on the future of mankind. All my life I have striven to awake my fellow Arthesians to their peril, but to no avail. They are lost in their giddy whirl of sensuous intoxication, of endless pleasures; my teachings will, however, bear eventual fruit. Of this I am assured by emissaries from the distant future, who inform me that I am the founder of the Arcadian Party, the first citizen of the Arcadian world that someday will be, and the first prophet of the Arcadian Age. My own remote descendant of the far-distant future, whom you know as the Lady Lis, has appeared to me many times. Most recently, she advised me of the forthcoming appearance of a man from the past—a man who will bear the key that can unlock mankind's prison—a man whose appearance in Arthex will be the salvation of the human race. I refer, of course, to yourself!"

Lux grinned feebly, not knowing how to react to this grandiose description of his role. He nodded, saying nothing, vaguely embarrassed to hear himself described in such tones of solemn grandeur.

Sonthus guided him through a gaudy maze of jumbled buildings and twisted streets.

"This world has doomed itself," the First Arcadian said quietly. "Its children dwindle from year to year, lost in their endless pursuit of pleasure, addicted to narcotic joys, losing memory of the former greatness of their race. Your arrival in this epoch represents freedom for mankind and the end of an age. I, perhaps, shall not live to see that sylvan utopia of the future, but I am proud that my teachings, which thus far have fallen on deaf ears, shall someday be proven wise. Helpless am I, alone and friendless, to oppose the massive might of the City Brain, or the cold egoism of Malaire. You alone can act to break this impasse between the Living City and the Weapon Machine, John Lux; but to do so you must first gain control over your own remarkable powers of body and mind . . . of this we shall converse later . . . now you shall rest and refresh yourself, safe for a time."

The house of Sonthus was on a little-traveled side street. It was a domed structure of creamy ceramic, adorned with stripes of brick red. They entered through a circular portal that opened in curved segments, like the iris of a camera. The novelty was lost on Lux, however, for sudden fatigue overwhelmed him, leaving him groggy and yearning for sleep.

Sonthus guided him through the iris portal into a central rotunda, sparsely decorated and dimly lit, where rows of worn, ancient books reposed in wall niches, and art objects that were doubtless of considerable antiquity stood about on pedestals. Among them Lux blurrily noticed a few representative pieces from his own age.

The house was cozy and warm and comfortable, but almost Spartan in its austere lack of decoration.

"Here you will be safe, at least for a time," Sonthus said. He indicated a room off the central foyer. "This will be yours. Later, we will talk; but now, you are fatigued. Bathe, rest, refresh yourself."

Lux found the 200,000 A D. version of a shower quite a novelty. Sonthus demonstrated its use, then left him to his own devices. It was a bubble of milky plastic with a round door. Lux stripped off his travel-stained clothes and entered the 'fresher-stall as Sonthus had called it. It was rather like climbing into a bathysphere in his own age.

Once in, he waved his hand before a luminous panel, following his host's example. Jets of rich, creamy lather covered him from head to foot, followed by piercing sprays of some scented astringent. It bothered Lux only slightly that he could not see the orifices from which the foam and spray jets came. When the astringent spray had washed away the lather, the jets turned themselves off. Next followed similarly sourceless blasts of warm, ultra-dry air that dried his body most efficiently. He emerged feeling deliciously clean.

Not wishing to don his soiled clothing right away, Lux wrapped himself in a voluminous robe of wooly material he found hanging on a wall peg behind the 'fresher-stall. He was engaged in removing the stubble from his jaws with a foamy, pine-scented depilatory when Sonthus entered, bearing a small tray. Ceramic cups and a beaker of some hot, creamy, nourishing drink like hot cocoa were on the tray.

The older man offered him a cup of the delicious beverage, and Lux sipped it gratefully, while waiting for the depilatory to dissolve his beard stubble. The drink was rich, sweet, and steaming hot. It sent a wave of warmth through Lux's weary body; he could feel the tension and fatigue draining from him. They talked a little of the current situation in Arthex.

"The race has lost itself in a giddy round of amusements," Sonthus said grimly. "In part this is a mode of escape from the suspense of continual warfare. It has caused incalculable psychic harm to man's self-esteem, the Ten-Thousand-Year Siege. The situation can no longer be permitted to continue. The Weapon Machine *must* succeed in breaking through the defenses of the City Brain! And soon . . . time is running out for humanity."

Lux nodded, stifling a yawn. Suddenly he felt very, very sleepy. Sonthus observed his inattention, and smiled.

"But we can discuss these matters when you are rested," he said. He indicated an adjoining cubicle, which served as a bedroom. "Sleep as long as you wish, John Lux. In my home you are safe from disturbance or scrutiny. In the morning—a term we still use from sheer historical habit, although it has long since lost all meaning for us here, living as we do under the eternal daylight of our artificial illuminants—when you awaken, we will explore the subject further, and set up a regimen."

"A regimen? For what?"

"You must gain conscious control of your neuro-radionic powers, first," Sonthus told him. "Then we will see if even your superhuman abilities are sufficient to destroy the Null Sphere and thus permit the Weapon Machine to fulfill its decamillennial purpose. But now—to your rest!"

He murmured a ceremonial phrase and left, the door to Lux's suite irising shut behind him.

Lux yawned again, threw off the wooly robe, and climbed wearily into his bed. He was much too worn out to pay any particular attention to the fact that the mattress was a self-inflating envelope of silky-warm, air-tight cloth. A bed was a bed to one as weary as he.

The sourceless illumination died away to darkness the moment he stretched out. In seconds he was sound asleep.

Afterward, he was never quite certain what it was that had awakened him. He found himself suddenly wide awake, and distinctly uneasy. Dismissing his mood as the result of imagination, he composed himself for sleep, but sleep did not come.

On sudden impulse he arose from the bed. The sourceless illumination banished the darkness of the room as soon as he had risen. He looked about, searching for something that resembled a bureau. It would seem the citizens of Arthex slept in the nude; at least, Sonthus had not supplied him with anything resembling pajamas, and his own garments, ragged and filthy, had vanished as soon as he had left the bathroom—perhaps carried away for laundering by an automatic servant.

He found no bureau, but a section of the wall irised open, displaying shelves lined with neatly folded garments of various descriptions. Lux settled on baggy culottes of electric blue and a ruffled blouse of royal purple. Heelless slippers, their toes decorated with puffs of white satin, completed his hasty costume. He left his room and prowled cautiously through the house, wary of stumbling over unseen obstacles in the darkness. But the house itself was determined to protect him, it seemed, for each room illuminated itself automatically as he entered it.

The murmur of low voices from a salon caught his attention. He didn't care to interrupt Sonthus in conversation, not knowing how to explain his presence here uncoached, and—for that matter—being unfamiliar with whatever language this future age spoke.

Suddenly it came to him in a burst of realization that Sonthus had greeted him in 20th-century English when he had accosted Lux in the street the night before. For some reason the anomaly of this had not penetrated to him at the time—doubtless fatigue and tension had dulled his intellect—but now, refreshed and rested from a few hours' deep sleep, he realized that it was hardly likely the people of 200,000 A.D. would speak any language recognizable to a person of his own day.

And it also occurred to him, almost in the same moment, that there was something vaguely familiar about Sonthus: not only his features, but the way he spoke. A haunting sense of having seen and heard Sonthus somewhere before came to him with the impact of a positive conviction, although he knew it was not possible.

He lingered near the door, trying to catch a glimpse of Sonthus and his unknown visitor. The salon was a bowl-shaped, sunken room, floored in some resilient red-brown substance like sponge rubber, the walls pierced with grilled, circular openings. The grills or lattices were vertical slats, like venetian blinds, and most of them were shut, but he found one that was partway ajar, and from this vantage he peered into the room and saw Sonthus, standing with his back turned, deep in conversation with a woman whose face was in the shadow of a hanging art-object of some kind.

As he peered in, the visitor was completing a remark.

"Tomorrow is too risky, with the Crisis Point only twelve hours away," she said forcefully. "He must be lured into the energy trap at once—now, tonight, if possible. *You must make every attempt to destroy him now.*"

As the astounding implications of this statement went thundering through his brain, the woman speaker leaned forward, laying her hand on Sonthus's forearm as if in emphasis. As she did so, her face came into the light, and with a shock of amazement he recognized the person who had just commanded his destruction.

It was the Lady Lis!

Lux shrank back behind the slats so as not to be seen. But at that same moment, Sonthus turned away from Lis, as if racked by indecision, and Lux got a clear look at him as well. He no longer wore what was now revealed as a hairpiece, and without those startlingly silver locks, and the neatly-trimmed imperial as well, Lux recognized him, too.

If anything, the shock of recognition was even more devastating.

It was Dr. Jonas Havering!

VIII. *The Great Secret*

JOHN LUX stumbled away from the salon, his mind a seething chaos of unanswered questions. Into the central foyer of the house, from which all rooms branched, he went swiftly, in confusion.

If the Lady Lis actually was, and had been all the while, his enemy, then he was in deadly danger every moment he remained in the house of her confederate. That Havering, too, was a denizen of the future was a revelation whose implications his mind could not yet fully grasp. But it was rapidly becoming clear that he had been misinformed all this while as to the true identity of his foes: it would seem the Arcadians of the distant future had been out to destroy him all along, and not the mysterious personage Malaire, whom he had yet to encounter.

Or could it be that both Malaire and Lis simultaneously sought his destruction? He pondered this possibility for a few moments. Had the two earlier attempts on his life been designed to drive him into the power of his supposed friend, Jonas Havering? Was it Lis or Malaire who had been the motivating force behind those first two attempts to kill him? If Havering was only a creature of the Arcadians, why had Lux not been drugged, poisoned, or slain while in Havering's house?

This chance discovery—that the Lady Lis was no friend of his, but in actuality one of his enemies, seeking his destruction—shook him to the core.

During their one brief meeting, he had been impressed with the young woman. Not only had he found her immensely attractive—physically desirable, in fact—but her character and personality had struck him as remarkable. Her brilliant dark eyes, alive with intelligence, bright with alertness; her perfect features, denoting strength of character and splendid breeding; the superior intellect that illuminated her wide brow and delicately chiseled face, aglow with intensity—everything about her had lingered in his mind. She had seemed to him the summation of everything he found interesting in a Woman—will, strength, vivid personality, brilliant intellect. To discover her now revealed as one of his foes dashed his speculations concerning the futurewoman.

But the overheard conversation had even more serious implications. Now that he knew she desired and actively sought his destruction, he would be forced to reevaluate each item of information she had given him that long-ago night she had so unexpectedly materialized in his room at Havering's house.

For example—did Arthex require destruction for the reasons she had supplied? Or had she some other, unrevealed reason for wishing the demolition of the Living City? Already, his own observations had ratified her stated opinions: he, too, had concluded the City was a beautiful, gaudy, ultimately deadly trap from which the remnants of mankind must be freed if the race was not to devolve into a soft, spineless group of helpless and decadent weaklings. But what were her real reasons for seeking to destroy Arthex—if, indeed, she did?

He felt cramped with frustration, the free play of his mind constrained. What, of the many things the futurewoman had told him, was truth?

Was any of it?

Another thought occurred to him. She had named his chief enemy to be the master of Arthex himself; but was this truth, or just another lie?

He mused on the fact, as yet, he had not even encountered this mystery man they called Malaire— this enigmatic being whose date or condition of birth even the scrupulous scientific geniuses of 1,000,-000 A.D. had not been able to discover.

Was Malaire his enemy?

Was Malaire the blind despot the Lady Lis had claimed him to be—the power-maddened dictator who held the dwindling remnants of a once-mighty civilization his pleasure-drunk slaves? Or could it perhaps be that actually Malaire labored tirelessly to free mankind from its jeweled prison—*which Lis opposed!*

Lux shrugged, tense with frustration. He gave up the attempt to wrestle with this tangle of irreconcilable questions as futile. But one thing was clear: he must flee this house at once! He did not know what the Lady Lis had meant by the phrase "energy trap," but it had a lethal sound to it. He had no desire to stay here and find out just *how* lethal!

He headed for the front entrance; it was closed when he came up to it, the iris sealed tightly. And he could not see any dial or handle or lever or lock by which it might be opened. He poked and pushed and prodded it awhile, and examined its circular frame, but, however it was locked, it resisted his every attempt to open it.

Remembering that his sleeping chamber had a window, he headed back to his room hurriedly. No sound came from the salon, but he would have seen if Lis or Sonthus had left it, so he was forced to assume that they were still deep in conversation.

Entering his room, he went directly to the window. It was shielded by flexible drapes of some plastic or other synthetic fabric in bright primary colors, and it looked like a shower curtain from his own time, except that the bottom edge of the drapery adhered somehow to the material of the wall, perhaps by magnetic attraction. He tried but could not pull the bottom edge of the drapery up, but they parted and pulled aside easily enough. He leaned out to survey the street—and got another surprise.

The house, which had been at street level when he had entered it, was now perhaps *a quarter of a mile in the air!*

Craning out precariously, he saw that it had risen on a thick tube or metal shaft of some kind. He had not the slightest idea why this had been done, unless as a precaution against his escaping from the house.

A mood of reckless daring possessed him. Thus far, Lis and Havering/Sonthus had been manipulating him, his thoughts and actions, as if he were a puppet and they the unseen, all-powerful puppet-masters. Well, this puppet was about to cut the strings—

Climbing up onto the sill, he jumped out of the room!

For the first second or two, he fell lazily, spinning down through the air, the wind whistling past him. The devil-may-care feeling of acting entirely on his own was heady—exhilarating. He had no particular fear of dashing his brains out against the glossy pavement below, confident his unconscious survival mechanism would teleport him to safety once he had reached the point of real danger.

But he had failed to take into account the motherly over-protectiveness of the Living City—

A metal arm extruded with lightning swiftness from the wall of the building opposite him, which was a slender, tapering mosquelike structure of striped orange and green glass, topped with a dome like the bulb of an onion, but colored virulent yellow.

From the tip of the armlike extension of a mass of steely, glittering tendrils whipped. These swirled about him as he fell to their level, and wove themselves together into a springy net. The net broke his fall effectively, knocking the wind out of him, and left him a helpless captive, dangling a hundred feet above the street, with no way to get down.

Perspiration broke out on his brow as Lux examined his predicament. The gyre of artificial luminaries still hovered far up in the black dome of the sky, still pouring their brassy radiance upon the city. Still the throng of celebrants surged through the streets, and he was exposed to the gaze of any who might glance skyward. And what of the artificial intelligence that powered and maintained the Living City, and kept watch over its childlike inhabitants? Surely the City Brain would be informed that the protective nets had snared a would-be suicide! And once Lux came under the scrutiny of the all-powerful mechanical intelligence, either it or its ally, Malaire, would know him for the quarry their Silver Men had followed to this century.

He strove in vain to extricate himself from the clinging mesh, but—perhaps purposefully—it seemed to resist his attempts to free his limbs.

Aircars like shining transparent bubbles floated through the sky over Arthex, drifting aimlessly to and fro, bearing the Arthesians from one pleasure or party to another. At any moment, one of these floating vehicles might notice his plight and summon whatever civic guard monitored the behavior of the citizens. Lux had jumped from the frying pan into the fire; he might have been wiser to have remained in the clutches of Havering/Sonthus, for all his intentions of subjecting him to this "energy trap," whatever it might turn out to be! Surely, whatever attempt was made on his life in the energy trap, he could teleport effortlessly to safety . . .

While these thoughts went through his mind, Lux noticed that one of the aircars had detached itself from the central stream and was floating towards him. As it came nearer, he saw that the bubblelike machine was larger than he had thought at first: this one was as huge as a transcontinental truck, and was partially opaque. It circled near, coming to rest in mid-air just beyond the perimeter of the net. He eyed it mistrustfully.

An invisible force plucked at him!

The intermeshed metallic strands parted reluctantly, as if countermanded by an external and superior force.

He swung loose of the net, floating in the grip of unseen force rays. A black portal irised into being in the underbelly of the aircar. The force beam drew him within, into darkness. Then the force fell away and he sprawled on a metal floor; behind him, somewhere, the iris closed.

Lux stood up; the huge vehicle was moving again, but he had no idea of the direction in which it was traveling, or of its height. He felt his way along smooth, cool metal walls without encountering any obstacle. He seemed to be in a circular chamber some twenty feet across.

A few moments later the cubicle brightened with that same soft, sourceless illumination-effect he had seen in the house of Havering/Sonthus. Now that he could see his surroundings, he saw that his first impressions of them had been correct in every detail. The iris had vanished; seemingly, the wall itself had contracted to hide it. Nor could he find any other exit to the circular room whatever.

It was a very effective prison.

A few moments after this, a panel of the curving wall glowed with light—blurred with colors—and drew into focus. It was either some kind of window, made of the same metallic substance as the rest of the wall, or a televisor of some kind.

Jonas Havering looked out at him, smiling amiably.

The picture, or whatever it was, was totally real, down to the last detail of shade and coloring, and complete with a three-dimensional depth effect.

Lux folded his arms, and regarded his "friend" impassively.

Havering did something with his hands that Lux could not see, as the "frame" of the picture cut off Havering's hands from view. A portion of the wall below the living-picture blurred and became covered with dials.

Lux went over and studied them. The wall had gone transparent in a long rectangular panel, revealing the bank of instruments. He was able to recognize several of them: there was a potentiometer, which measured electric force, a sort of thermometer to record temperature changes, and what looked like a Geiger counter. Unable to ascertain anything further, he stepped back to the center of the circular room and looked up at Jonas Havering—for, whatever his actual name or identity might prove to be, Lux could not help but think of him as Havering.

A grim smile touched the lips of his captor.

"Evidently you overheard a portion of our conversation," said Havering. The sound must have been broadcast into the room by a concealed speaker; if so, it sounded completely natural and without any distortion effects.

"Evidently," Lux murmured.

"Then you will be aware of our intentions," the other commented. "Very well, it matters little. The nature of the energy trap will become obvious to you shortly. *You will now be subjected to every harmful intensity of energy known to man, in our last attempt to destroy you.*"

The screen blanked out and became a wall of featureless metal again.

A split second later, a bolt of lightning leaped out of the wall and flashed towards him!

Lux was teleported the length of the cubicle before the fountain of electric fire could touch him. It splashed harmlessly off the insulated metal and vanished, leaving a strong odor of ozone behind.

Another bolt speared at him—and another! Each time his survival mechanism teleported him out of the zone of danger.

Lux began to wonder why this meaningless charade was being enacted. Surely his captor knew he could teleport out of the path of any danger. Then why these futile attempts to destroy him?

He waited tensely, but no further bolts of electric flame came flashing toward him. Instead he became aware of a growing sensation of heat. He glanced toward the panel of instruments beneath the place where the living picture had been. As he had guessed, the temperature recorder registered steadily increasing heat levels within the windowless cubicle of insulated metal. He wiped his brow, conscious of perspiration trickling down his sides. But this was ludicrous—surely although trapped and helpless, Havering/Sonthus did not expect him to simply remain here and roast to death! Surely, when the temperature became unendurable, he could simply teleport to safety—outside the flying car.

As if somehow tuned in to his thoughts, this captor said:

"Not so, John Lux! Hasn't it occurred to you yet that your teleportational abilities are limited to line-of-sight? When you were in the plane, back in your own age, and the Silver Men were pursuing you —why do you think you couldn't teleport to safety?"

Perspiration burst out on Lux's face. Was Havering/Sonthus right? He remembered that moment in the airplane cabin; he had visualized a certain familiar spot in Weston and had striven to teleport himself there—and had failed.

"And that time, trapped in the taxicab, sinking in the river," the voice taunted, "again you tried to teleport to safety—and failed! *Don't you realize, you fool, that you can only teleport to a scene within eyesight!* You cannot escape from this aircab, because you do not know where you are. Your present location and altitude, velocity, and direction are unknown to you. And you cannot *see out.*"

Perspiration was rolling down Lux now; his garments were soaked. The air was stifling, bakingly hot, like the breath from an open furnace. The soles of his slippers were blisteringly hot, and the stench of their scorching plastic soles was thick in his nostrils. He gasped for breath—

"Why are you doing this to me—why?" he panted.

"Think, John Lux! *Think!* In a few moments the temperature in the cubicle will be beyond human endurance!"

Why that strange note of urgency in the voice of one trying with every means at his command to kill him?

And who was the mysterious personage whom he had known back in his own far-distant era as Jonas Havering, and who here was named Sonthus? Was he the agent of Lis and the Arcadians—or of Malaire, the faceless and yet-unmet master of Arthex? Or was he some agent of the Weapon Machine itself? In the long millennia of its strange war against Arthex, had the cold artificial intelligence that powered the gigantic aerial fortress of indestructible metal somehow evolved the power of independent thought?

The temperature rose steadily. Lux gasped for

breath—and each inhalation dried the tissues of his mouth. Sweat streamed down into his eyes, blurring his vision. The urgency of his predicament was perfectly obvious. Unless he somehow managed to escape from this place of torment, he was doomed. Extinction lay mere minutes away!

He turned his attention inward, down into the depths of his being. He searched there for something he could not name. The survival mechanism that existed on the level of the human unconscious would protect him to the utlimate limit. *But what was that limit?*

And then, suddenly, *he knew!*

The Great Secret was his, shock reverberated throughout his being as the inmost secrets of his power were laid bare to him. He gasped in utter amazement, exploring the new power that now lay open in his grasp.

"Hurry, John Lux! The heat rise is now at the upper endurance level of human life!" the voice thundered.

But Lux paid it no heed—in fact, did not even hear the words that echoed through the chamber, whose superheated air shimmered now with waves of intolerable heat.

Of course! He should have known—should have guessed! The only means left to his survival mechanism in such circumstances was to divulge to his conscious mind the technique of operating his hidden brain centers!

It was like a long-sealed door opening . . . or a great dam parting! Knowledge flooded into his conscious mind; like a blueprint spread out before him, he saw exactly how his neuro-radionic powers worked, and how his brain could tap, control, and manipulate the various forms of radiant energy.

The revelation was an astounding one.

It was also incommunicable. He knew with utter certainty that he could never teach another person how to do the trick. Can a brilliant Grand Master ever put into words how he anticipates with lightning speed the multi-valued implications of each chess play? Can a great musician ever explain to another the instinctive grasp he attains of a piece of music—the vision of overall totality, the warp and woof of a classic symphony?

No, the Great Secret was beyond the power of mere words to express. Language could not convey it; even the rarefied upper strata of higher mathematics could never depict or describe that amazingly simple yet infinitely complex pattern of thought.

"Lux! Lux! The temperature is beyond that at which life can exist—"

The words shouting through the broiling cubicle penetrated to his enthralled consciousness. Almost absently, Lux reached out—with a portion of his mind whose existence he had never realized until now—reached out in a certain manner no other human being could ever duplicate, or even comprehend—took hold of the searing heat-energy—and turned it aside.

It became measurably cooler.

To his enhanced vision, it was as if the fundamental nature of the heat waves was a visible thing, like a structure or a pattern.

With an extension of his new mind, he took hold of this pattern and—diverted it? Rechanneled it? Negated it? Verbal communication does not contain a label for what he did, any more than the sciences that study the human mind contain an explanation of how he did it.

The temperature dropped. Became normal.

And Lux awaited the next act in the attempt to destroy him.

It was not long in coming.

IX. *The Central Ziggurat*

JOHN LUX became aware of a faint tingling sensation in the nerves of his body. The irritant was negligible, but it was there. He could not at once put a name to the phenomenon, but he knew that some kind of energy was being directed against him.

Puzzled, he took another look at the panel of instruments. None of them was registering anything, except for the device he had tentatively designated as resembling a Geiger counter. On that dial, the indicator bar was creeping through the yellow danger zone into the red zone, that of killing intensity.

He was being bombarded with gamma radiation!

He frowned slightly. Again he employed his curious propensity to visualize energy flows. Heat waves he had seen as spreading concentric circles of dull, luminous crimson. But now gamma radiation appeared to his new senses like floating rods of weird purple phosphorescence.

He traced the slow-moving bars to their source, grilles of power-impregnated metal set in the ceiling of the insulated chamber. Reaching out in an indescribable way, he did something to those dim luminous bars of deadly radiation. They ceased coming.

Lux looked around, jubilantly. He wondered what form of energy might be used against him next. Whichever it was, he was fully confident of his new-found ability to harness and divert it.

A vast excitement had seized him; exultation sang through his veins like rare wine. He had stumbled upon knowledge of a sort no man had ever possessed before him . . . and it was a fortunate accident that his background and training were such as to have prepared him to utilize the secret he had learned, and to swiftly grasp the practical mechanics of his self-discovery.

For, back in his own remote age, John Lux had started as a scientist, trained in the employment of electronic forces. His brilliant grasp of theoretical physics, his intuitive but disciplined imagination, had enabled him to visualize—experiment—design. Patents had flowed from him, bringing millions within his grasp. A rare sense of practical business methods had made it possible for him to capitalize on his discoveries, and to erect a multimillion-dollar industrial empire on a handful of subelectronic inventions.

But had this freak accident of genetics, this unique mutation, fallen to the lot of another, it was more than likely that, lacking any specific scientific training in the forces and potentials of the electromagnetic spectrum, the other superman would have been helpless to utilize his discoveries so swiftly. Another man would have died there in the energy trap; Lux lived!

And waited for the next attack to come.

Each assault made on him so far had employed one or another intensity of common energy. He knew that all varieties of radiant energy are merely different forms of the same basic force. Heat had been applied through the agency of infrared rays, a form of energy spread over nine octaves of the common electromagnetic spectrum, with very low quantum energies—below one electron volt, in fact. He had rendered the infrared beams harmless without effort.

The gamma rays, were, however, of a different and higher order of energy. Gamma radiation is near the top of the spectrum, covering eight octaves, with wavelengths of up to one thousand Siegbahn units, and quantum energies ranging up to one million electron volts.

Thus far, he knew, he was able to handle energy flows covering nearly one third of the electromagnetic spectrum. He speculated as to how much energy he could control. What was next in the order of attack? Cosmic rays? Quite probably—and could he handle energies in that range of intensity? For the cosmics have quantum energies of staggering immensity. Toward the top of the cosmic-ray octaves, he knew, he would be handling quantum forces ranging up to eighty-two *billion* electron volts!

Could he control forces of that awesome magnitude? Could any merely human being, however mutated, channel and manipulate forces in *that* range?

In the control cabin of the aircar, the man John Lux had known as Jonas Havering studied the flickering signal lights on the indicator board before him with a mixture of awe and delight.

"He has done it!" he exclaimed to his companion. "Achieved conscious control of his neuro-radionic power—amazing!"

"Cosmic radiation is next, I believe," the Lady Lis said, tersely.

"Yes; if he can handle that kind of energy, he can cope with anything." Havering's hand manipulated the all-purpose energy projector, turning the dial settings to broadcast waves of force at frequencies of 10^{24} cycles per second, at wavelengths of a few thousandths of one angstrom unit, in the eighty-billion-electron-volt range of quantum energy.

He thrust home the red trigger.

Nothing happened.

"Something's gone wrong!" Lis exclaimed. "He is not grasping the energy flow—or is not able to!"

Dismay was etched on Havering's features.

"You are right . . . the chamber is bathed in deadly radiation . . . and he is doing nothing about it. Nothing at all!"

"Quick—take a visual check."

Havering nodded, and manipulated the controls of the televisor.

A moment later a cry of astonishment escaped from his lips.

For the chamber was empty.
John Lux had—vanished!

Hanging unsupported in mid-air above the colorful metropolis, John Lux watched the aircar hurtle away from him. In a few seconds it dwindled and disappeared, lost amid the stream of traffic. A brief smile lightened his features. He could picture the amazement, the consternation, of those who had thought him imprisoned in an escape-proof trap—finding him gone, escaped from their power after all!

He had seen no particular reason to remain any longer as a guinea pig, awaiting shower after shower of ever-deadlier energies. Now that he had attained conscious command of his rare talents, he was determined to become the master of his own actions once again.

For too long he had dangled like a puppet from on a string, helpless in the grip of an unseen puppet-master. From now on, *he* was the captain of his own destiny.

Perhaps Jonas Havering had been correct in saying that his ability to teleport was limited to line of sight. But that was only true of his powers in the latent stage! His experience in traversing the Null Sphere had suggested to him that when he teleported it was something other than mere dematerialization. If that had been the truth, dematerialized or not, he would still have been irremediably destroyed when projecting himself through the black zone of distorted pseudospace.

Since he had not been destroyed in entering the Living City, then it was obvious that the secret of teleportation was not just dematerialization. It could only be that his mind somehow bent space itself!

Thus, rather than remain in the energy trap, waiting to resist the next attack, he had attempted to teleport himself *outside* the aircar, into mid-air. He had succeeded.

And this time he was conscious of exactly what

happened during the split second of teleportation. What happened was a very peculiar experience. In an indescribable manner, he reached out with an extension of his mind and "took hold" of the very fabric of the space/time continuum in two places.

He could not help thinking of the act except in physical terms. Space/time was a mesh of interwoven forces, like a fishnet. Reaching out with both hands, let us say. he grasped two different parts of the net—and bent them together so that, very briefly, the two different "places" simultaneously coexisted, or at least overlapped. For a fleeting fraction of a second, his body occupied simultaneously two different areas of space.

The state of coexistence was unnatural; it was a strain on the very fabric of space/time, and the region of bent and overlapping space *must* spring apart again, restoring equilibrium to the warped fabric. When that happened, his body had a choice of either remaining in its original location or occupying the second location.

All Lux did was merely increase his body's potential for continuing to occupy the second location.

Thus he flickered out of existence in one place, and flickered into existence in another—*without actually passing through the intervening region.*

This being the case, he did not have to operate within line of sight at all. That limitation had been imposed upon him by his survival mechanism, which as a function of his unconscious mind was by definition not capable of conscious thought or reason. It refused to precipitate him blindly into an unknown location, which might well also be a place of danger. But when his ability to teleport came under the control of the "awake" portion of his brain, this self-imposed limitation was within his power to negate. For a man can consciously thrust himself into danger, or risk his life on a gamble.

He had flashed into being several hundred yards beyond the curved, glittering hull of Havering's flying vehicle. For the first few moments, he had fallen through the air, helpless as a stone, helpless in the omnipresent grip of gravity.

But gravity itself, he discovered, is but another form of radiant energy, and although the science of Lux's age had yet to find a place for it on the chart of electromagnetic forces, his superhuman sensory powers were able to reach out and "grasp" the nature and the substance of the gravitational forces.

To his extraordinary inner vision, gravity waves appeared as a dim blue pulsating glow, welling from beneath him, one throbbing beat rising to blend with another. He realized that the energy flow of gravitation was unlike the other forces which he had manipulated thus far. The forces he had previously dealt with had wavelengths that were incredibly small. The wavelengths of the infrared rays, for example, had been about one thousand Siegbahn units. That is an indescribably minute interval of space— only one hundred-millionth of a centimeter apart.

In a word, infrared light moves in waves, and those waves are only one hundred-millionth of a centimeter apart.

Gravity waves are vastly different, he perceived. The distance between those deep, slow waves is one of almost inconceivable vastness—*the width of the entire solar system!*

The quantum energy of gravitational forces, too, was a strange, inverse thing—a *negative* energy, he saw, although he could not fully understand how that could be. But below the narrow range of visible light, he realized, the quantum energies are *reversed.* And as gravity waves are very far down the spectrum from light waves, way down below radar and television and radio frequencies, this weird *negative* electron voltage was in the range of minus many thousand billion electron volts.

Despite the utter strangeness of the gravity waves, he found himself able to grasp and manipulate the energy flow, and thus he arrested his fall before he had descended more than a thousand feet, and hung suspended.

The sensation must be the same as astronauts experience in free fall, he conjectured. Weightlessness does peculiar things to the inner ear, and uncomfortable things to the stomach. But he mastered the discomfort he felt, and began to think about what he should do next.

It would not be long before his erstwhile captor discovered that he had eluded his prison and came circling back, hoping to scoop him up again. Lux felt certain he would have no particular difficulty in escaping from the clutches of Jonas Havering for the second time, but saw no value in repeating the exploit. And it just might be that Havering had a trick or two left; after all, Havering had carefully anticipated this course of events, and his planning might extend to including among his armaments a method of immobilizing Lux, or rendering him unconscious.

Lux decided not to risk it.

He would find a place to land at once; every moment he remained aloft increased the chances that Havering would return to attempt his recapture.

The building nearest to where Lux hovered weightlessly in space was a colossal structure at the center of the gaudy metropolis. On impulse, Lux "lowered" himself toward it; that is, he gradually permitted a small percentage of the gravitational waves to affect his mass, thus pulling him downward.

Floating gently down, Lux studied the enormous edifice curiously. It was built as a system of tremendous square levels, which grew smaller as the structure increased in height, each tier set back from the one beneath. It reminded him of illustrations he had once seen in a textbook on archeology. In a moment the caption that had been printed beneath the illustration came into his memory: "The step-pyramid of Sakkara." He recalled the text had compared the basic design of the pyramid to the ziggurats of ancient Babylon.

Towards this central ziggurat, then, he descended. As he neared, he experimented gingerly with various methods of directing his descent into a controlled flight. The ziggurat, he observed, had a steely sheen to it, as if it were sheathed in metal. If it was constructed of a ferrous metal, Lux reasoned, it might have a magnetic field about it—which meant he should be able to manipulate that field.

Reaching out with his curious new sensory apparatus, Lux attuned his vision to the frequency of magnetic force, and observed that his reasoning had been correct. The steel structure emitted a faint magnetic field, which he "saw" as a dim haze of pale, vague, reddish luminance. Reaching out and grasping the essential pattern of the magnetic field, he discovered he could temporarily change the charge from positive to negative.

Arresting his flight, he hovered some eight yards away from the nearest tier of the step-pyramid, his brow creased in thought. It was singularly humiliating, but the extraordinary superman who could rebuff lightning and harness the eerie force of gravitation could not for the moment remember the simplest fact about magnetism—whether it is like poles that attract and unlike poles that repel, or vice versa!

In a moment he relaxed, grinning self-consciously, as he managed to recall that it is unlike poles which attract. He manipulated the magnetic field of the building and built a field up around himself, making the ziggurat field positive and his own field negative. Magically, he floated toward the tier, and managed to set down, a bit jerkily, on a balcony outside of tall, narrow windows. He touched solid metal and relaxed the fields; a wild, heady feeling of utter exhilaration passed through him. He felt ready to take on the universe itself, and his jaunty mood of supreme self-confidence was perhaps excusable.

After all, in the past thirty seconds he had conquered a power that men had dreamed of for as far back as there were men to dream—the power of flying!

The windows were unfastened; he thrust them open, and stepped over the sill into a darkened room. He had not the faintest notion of where he was, but he felt no particular fear. He took a few more steps into the room. He was just beginning to wonder if he could not utilize his neuro-radionic powers to enable him to see in the dark, perhaps by means of self-produced radar waves, when a voice addressed him from the pitch darkness.

"Do not move, intruder! My weapon is heat-sensitive, and is trained directly upon you!"

He started violently at the unexpected words. The voice was that of a young woman, and, in surprising contrast to the hysteric, hedonistic citizens of Arthex he had thus far encountered, her tones were remarkably businesslike and competent.

However, he felt no alarm. Smiling faintly, he took another step, fully confident his powers could detect and nullify or turn aside whatever destructive energies might be directed at him.

"I warn you—*remain where you are or I fire!*"

The woman's voice came from directly in front of him, he decided. He could see nothing in the blackness, but continued on in the direction he had assumed.

"Very well then, idiot—"

He heard a faint hiss, as of a jet of air escaping from a narrow tube.

He tensed himself to receive and divert an energy flow.

In the next instance a peculiar odor assailed his nostrils. Vague alarm stirred through him. He opened his mouth as if to speak or cry out—and fell face forward into a thick, soft carpet. Numbness spread through him, and he sank into a deep slumber.

Before consciousness lapsed, however, a scathing thought flashed through his dimming brain.

You over-confident cretin—anesthetic gas!

Then he knew no more. After all, even a neuro-radionic superman is vulnerable to knockout gas . . .

X. *The City Master*

JOHN LUX was dimly aware of brilliant lights above him and of the sound of voices filled with urgency and of the touch of cold instruments here and there upon his body, but he drifted in a dreaming haze of euphoria, and it was as if these things were happening to some person other than himself.

A voice came out of the haze, a man's, young and puzzled:

"But how did he get into your suite, Azonna? Your apartments are on the twentieth level, and the City Brain automatically repulses any aircars from approaching the ziggurat—"

Another voice, that of a man's, but older, authoritative:

"As for that, the detectors would give the alarm if any car approached within one hundred meters—and none of the cattle possesses, or knows how to use, flying suits. An inexplicable mystery—how exciting!"

Cattle? Is that what they call the citizens? The question floated through Lux's mind lazily; he had suspected that some sort of ruling cadre must exist, for surely all of Arthex could not consist of the childlike carnival-goers he had seen romping through the streets, and Malaire could hardly be the one lone mature and intelligent Arthesian. But the information meant nothing to him in his dreamy, relaxed state; it merely registered on his consciousness.

"Look here, Hothar . . . notice the meter readings? This specimen of blood shows no addictions at all . . . and look at the mental level . . . he has full mental clarity. Why, he might even be one of us! Give me that potentiometer—"

Lux felt cold metal clamps press gently on his temples. Then a faint tingling went through his scalp: unpleasant, but too faint to rouse his slumbering senses to an awareness of pain.

Alarm and amazement sounded in the next voice, making it shrill:

"Great City! This man is a *primitive*—look at those synapses! Look at the development of the cortex! Level Two, I should hazard!"

"A throwback?" another voice questioned. "An atavism? But the Genetic Monitors would surely have reported such an anomalous birth. What is it we have here, anyway—a mutation of some sort?"

Another voice, lazy and drawling:

"I believe Coram has hit upon it; definitely some sort of mutation. Why, the omniometer shows his nervous system is developed ten million percent beyond the human norm! With a nervous system such as this, he should be able to manipulate pure energy throughout the electromagnetic spectrum! He's a neuro-radionic superman!"

"Omtar is accurate in his extrapolation," the older, more authoritative voice mused, "But Kayon is equally correct in gauging his evolutionary phase as Level Two, which would put him two hundred thousand years behind us—a mutation from the remote past, then?"

"Obviously," a woman's voice said, coldly. "I have just completed an entropy count of his molecular structure, while you fools gabbled like a pack of hysterical children. The man belongs to circa 2000 A.D., to use the old-fashioned chronology system. Malaire must be informed of our discovery at once: *This man is a time-traveler!*"

"Is it safe to just leave him here? Shouldn't we destroy him while he is helpless? Suppose he regains full consciousness—it is impossible to calculate the limits of his neuro-radionic powers . . . theoretically, he could destroy the City . . . destroy even the planet itself!"

Contempt was audible in the cold voice of the woman:

"Superman or not, he is helpless while in the euphoric state, and he will remain in that state so long as the machine continues to manipulate the pleasure centers of his brain. Come along!"

"But he could cancel out the machine, could he not!"

"*Of course* he could—but he won't! Will you do as I say: we must apprise Malaire of the presence of this time-traveling mutation at once."

What machine is it that they're talking about . . . oh, THAT machine, Lux thought lazily. He was aware, now that the voices had called his attention to its existence, of a mechanism near his head that monitored the alpha rhythm of his thought waves and kept bathing the pleasure centers of his brain in a mild stimulus; lazily, not really caring about it, he reached out with his powers almost playfully, and tampered with the waves of force bathing his brain—

and came fully awake!

Cold perspiration drenched him from head to foot as he realized with crawling horror the insidious spell that mind-neutralizing instrument had woven about him, sapping his will, immersing him in a dreamy haze of blissful euphoria.

He killed the machine's power cell with a lance of thought and, reaching out, seized the minds of the several Arthesians in the room with him. He did not waste time in disposing of them; insinuating himself into their minds, he seized control of the motor centers and slammed a burst of nervous energy through their brains. The Arthesian brains reacted to this extraordinary "overload" just as would any other sensitive and delicately balanced electrical instrument: they short-circuited.

The half-dozen Arthesian technicians collapsed on the elastic floor in a tangle of sprawling limbs. They would remain dead to the world for several hours. Lux had blown their mental fuses, so to speak.

These potential sources of difficulty removed, Lux then turned to examine his own condition. He discovered he had been stripped naked and his body now reclined on a platform of some warm resilient substance—a plastic of some kind, he surmised. He was not tied down by any straps, or by any other visible form of restraint, but some intangible force rendered him immobile. Numerous instruments were attached to various organs and nerve centers by metal tubes ending in flat discs, and these discs adhered to his body in some manner he did not comprehend.

He wasted no time in eliminating these restraints and encumbrances. He nullified the forces holding him to the metal platform, plucked the sucker-like attachments from his flesh, and hunted around for his clothing without finding any.

Shrugging, he decided to strip one of the unconscious technicians. They were a small-bodied lot with delicate, overbred features and large, mostly hairless skulls, men and women alike clad in close-fitting one-piece overalls of some silky gray cloth he could not identify. Over the left breast, these uniforms bore a scarlet emblem that bore no meaning Lux could discern: it looked halfway between Arabic script and a scribble.

Choosing the tallest of the male technicians. Lux undressed the man and donned the gray suit. He had quite a bit of trouble in figuring out the mode of fastening current in 200,000 A.D. The suit was held together somehow, but not by buttons, snaps, zippers, or any other mode known to him. Eventually losing patience, he inspected the man's garments by means of his radionic sensory powers and discovered that certain overlapping panels of the synthetic cloth adhered by electrostatic charges. Once he learned this, it was a simple thing to cancel out the electrostatic charge, thus loosening the suit. When he was dressed, he simply restored the charge. He also donned the gray slipper-like footwear the technician was wearing.

His hair might prove a problem, as the ruling cadre of the City seemed to tend generally toward baldness. The oldest of the technicians—probably the one the others had addressed as Hothar—wore a skullcap of gray felt, or some such warm fabric. He slipped it off the man's head and put it on his own; pulling it well down, he found it covered his hair.

Beyond the room where he had been examined by the technicians, he found himself in a long, high-ceilinged hallway. The floor covering was of the omnipresent elastic substance the people of 200,000 A.D. preferred to carpets, and the mode of lighting was the same sourceless illumination he had noticed in the house of Sonthus.

He turned and looked in both directions. The hallway was untenanted, save for himself; at one end it terminated in a lateral corridor, and at the other in what looked like a kind of rotunda, lined with transparent and perhaps hollow columns of tubes whose purpose he could not at once ascertain. On impulse, he headed off down the hallway toward the pillar-lined rotunda.

Innumerable irising portals lined the corridor to either side, all of them shut. He had no notion as to what activities might be going on behind them, and as the emblems painted to the right of each portal was in a complex script unknown to him, he could not even hazard a guess.

He was not particularly alarmed at the possibility that one of the Arthesian cadremen might come into the hall at any moment and discover a stranger, although he was not looking forward to the chances of such a meeting. Despite his foolhardy over-confidence, and the humiliation he had suffered at his capture, an hour or so earlier, by the woman technician, Azonna, armed with the gas gun, he nonetheless felt able to handle himself in whatever emergency situation might arise.

He was not, however, quite prepared for the interruption when it did come.

He was about halfway to the rotunda end of the corridor when one of the portals irised open and there emerged into view a remarkable figure.

It was manlike in shape and size, but it was not a man. Its body was of sleek, glistening blue metal, the torso molded all in one piece, the limbs overlapping sequences of metal rings, the head a featureless ovoid which bore no sensory apparatus of any kind. Stenciled or printed in some manner across the breast of the metal thing was another of those cryptic scarlet symbols which were, for him, devoid of meaning.

Lux strove to retain his composure, and to look upon the glistening thing with a semblance of calm. Such automata were doubtless commonplace here in the central ziggurat, for he had already deduced, from certain remarks he had overheard in his euphoric state from the conversation among the technicians, that this edifice housed the central government, or at least the human administration, of the Living City.

But he could not help gawking, all the same. Indeed, he probably would not have been completely human if he could have looked upon the gleaming robot unmoved. For here walked one of man's most ancient and unobtainable dreams—mechanical life.

Or, rather, *glided,* for the automaton flowed along with a supple, boneless grace that was fluid in its movement and of unearthly beauty. This was due, he supposed, to the essential differentness in the structure of its limbs. Man stalks along on stiff, jointed bones in an ungainly manner; the robot's legs were linked rings that slid against each other smoothly, held together by the adhesion of magnetic forces. Thus it did not exactly walk—but *flowed,* as a serpent flows.

As they passed in the hall, the automaton turned the featureless ovoid of its face as if to regard him.

It was an uncanny, even an unnerving experience, being stared at from an eyeless face. Lux almost felt as a tangible pressure the regard of those eyes that were not there. And he started uncontrollably when next addressed by a voice that came from God knows where. For the thing had no mouth, either.

"Salutation, Doctor!"

The voice was a tuneless humming, a droning song shaped into words. Once John Lux had heard an experimental voder—a machine that simulates spoken words without attempting to sound like an artificial human voice. It had sounded quite as completely inhuman as this song of metal.

"Salutation!" Lux returned briskly.

"You are doubtless bearing reports of the examination of the intruder who entered Central by the twentieth level," the automaton said. It sounded like a statement; at least, the singing hum did not imitate the rising inflection on the last word or two of the remark which habit gives to a question when humans converse.

"I am," Lux said—and it was not exactly a lie.

"The City Master impatiently waits upon your report and the results of your interview of the intruder," the metal being sang. "The private tube is waiting; you will, of course, have your insignia about your person."

Lux hesitated.

As before, the remark seemed as much a statement of fact as a query. Lux wondered what the robot meant by its queer use of the word *insignia*. Could it be that he was supposed to show some sort of credentials?

It suddenly crossed his mind that the machine man was most likely some sort of security guard or police monitor. A mere machine laborer, servitor, or message-bearer would hardly be likely to engage a chance-met human superior in a chat. It also occurred to him that such robots would make the best possible security guards; they neither wearied nor slept, needed no rest or refreshment; their attention would be unflagging, their vigilance unwavering, and their metallic bodies proof against assault and injury.

However, this thought merely crossed his mind, and it had no real bearing on the issue of the moment. Was the robot asking for some sort of identity card? It was impossible to tell. Lux decided to bluff it through; he could always, he assumed, immobilize the creature with a stunning blast of force if it attempted to halt him or to signal an alarm.

If he was able to "blow a fuse" in the neuronic patterns of human minds, he should certainly find it an easy task to do so in the brain of a robot!

"Oh, of course!" he said, affecting a casual tone, answering the statement/query.

The acknowledgment seemed to satisfy the automaton, for it nodded the sleek, featureless ovoid of its head, and without further conversation continued on its way down the corridor, moving with that fascinating fluid grace he had admired before.

Lux reached the rotunda at the terminus of the hallway and found it untenanted.

He examined the area curiously.

Nine transparent columns or tubes were set at evenly spaced intervals around the curve of the far wall. They were fashioned of some lucent material he could not identify. It did not seem to be either glass or crystal, although it was equally transparent; neither did it have the look or the feel of any plastic. The tube substance, in fact, seemed—to the touch, at least—to possess the relative density of metal.

The tubes were quite large in girth—large enough to accommodate a man, surely—and they ran from floor to ceiling. They were hollow, and, as they pierced the floor and the ceiling, they looked to Lux rather like some kind of elevator.

However, they were empty; no cage or even platform was visible. And search as he might, Lux could find no call buttons or any other form of controls.

The automaton had said, "The private tube is waiting." Did he expect Lux to step into a hollow shaft many stories above the street level? True, a panel stood open in the first tube of the row, but it gave upon vacancy—upon empty air!

Lux stood, biting his lip indecisively.

On sheer chance, he surveyed the seemingly empty shaft with his new sensory equipment. Much to his surprise, he detected an unceasing flow of energy waves moving upward at a leisurely rate. Probing more deeply into the pattern of the energy flow, he discovered that the structure of the force was sufficient to counteract the pull of gravity, propelling a person in the shaft to the levels above.

An anti-gravity elevator! he marveled.

It took a bit of persuasion, however, to voluntarily walk into the empty shaft, even though Lux was aware by now that his own powers included the ability to control gravitational forces. Old habits die hard, he found.

Steeling himself, he stepped forward into empty space—and found himself floating upward at a smooth, even acceleration! The transition from normal gravity to weightlessness had been perfectly unobtrusive, and the sensation was not in the least unpleasant.

After a second, the velocity at which he rose increased by the multiple of ten. He realized this only from the blurring rapidity with which the levels flashed past his gaze, but physically he felt none of the pressure he might have expected. Weightlessness gave a bodiless feeling, as if he had been divested of all inertia. He wondered at the thought, but only briefly. He was too filled with tension and anticipation to marvel over technological wonders.

For at last he was about to come face to face with the mysterious and potent individual who dominated the surviving remnants of mankind, here at the close of the Urban Age!

He was about to confront his unknown enemy at last—the shadowy enigma who had sought his death, who had hunted him through space and through time itself by means of the Silver Men!

In mere moments he would meet—*Malaire!*

XI.   *The Death Zone*

JOHN LUX extended his sensories, studying the force field which sustained his body in the empty shaft. By means of his remarkable new abilities he was able to perceive and to scrutinize the energy flow that pulsed through the length of the hollow transparent cylinder.

It was a counter-gravitic force new to him and essentially unlike the mode of travel he had used to fly to the central ziggurat hours before. At the time he had materialized in mid-air beyond the glassy hull of Havering's aircar, he had simply seized the power source of Earth's gravitational field, utilizing that energy flow to hold himself aloft. But the anti-gravity field in the "elevator" tube was of an entirely different order of electromagnetic force.

From somewhere at the base of the shaft—buried, perhaps, in the foundations of this structure, which the Arthesians themselves called *Central*—a powerful energy projector was housed. This instrument, he realized now that he studied the nature of the pattern of force it directed up the tube, did not so much cancel out or negate the gravity waves as it disregarded them. What it actually did (he perceived) was to project a field of force similar to a stasis field. This field bound the particles which made up the atomic structure of any material body which entered the shaft in a net of force. Thus cradled in the grip of a tenuous web of force, the atomic system was thrust up the shaft at a uniform rate of acceleration.

The energy projector did not fight against gravity: it circumvented it!

Despite the tension of the moment, and the excitement he felt in anticipation of his forthcoming confrontation with the mysterious City Master, John Lux could not help marveling at the extraordinary technical achievement this instrument represented.

And here again was visible and tangible proof of the decadence into which the human race had fallen in this deadend called the Urban Age. In a healthier, more free epoch, when the instinct to pioneer and explore had not been suppressed to the point of being all but bred out of mankind, such an invention would have pointed the pathway to the stars.

For the gravitic engine struck the shackles from man, liberating him from that one prison that was older even than the Living City—the planet itself.

But here in the pleasure city of Arthex, the magnificent invention that could have lifted the race to the stars, could have spread mankind throughout the galaxy and the universe itself, was used—as an elevator!

Despite the fact that both the Lady Lis and the enigmatic individual who was known as Jonas Havering in one eon and Sonthus of Arthex in another were seemingly his foes, with yet-unexplained designs on his very life, Lux became increasingly convinced with every passing hour he spent in this gilded prison-city that the cause in which they had sought to enlist his aid was a just one.

Did that mean that Malaire, as well, was his foe?

Malaire, too, had sought his destruction through the Silver Men, his tireless hunters.

Were all three of them his enemies?

Or could it be that Malaire was his friend?

As yet, it was impossible for the neuro-radionic superman to reach a decision on this overwhelmingly important question. He lacked sufficient information upon which to base even a cursory deduction as to the hidden and secret motives of those three mysterious individuals, Lis, Havering/Sonthus, and Malaire.

But within mere moments he would stand face to

face with the most mysterious of the three, and would force the answers to some of those questions from him.

The scientific curiosity that had impelled him to probe into the energy flow that powered the anti-gravitic elevator tube saved the life of John Lux a fraction of a second later.

His sensories still extended, he suddenly perceived that the gravity-resisting flow of force was lifting him into a zone of inimical energy.

Ahead of him, up the shaft, his sensories observed a curious pattern of force. To his energy-sensitive inner vision it resembled a shimmering flow of fiery blue ripples. This blur of overlapping impulses, he discovered in a lightning-swift probe, was a complex system of heterodyning fields. This pattern of electromagnetic force was being broadcast on the frequencies of human thought-waves, and would jam any human mind within range. The principle was the same as that in which a burst of Hertzian waves are used to jam a radio.

The pattern would cause mental interference and then dysfunction in any sentient brain, even a robot's.

And he was rapidly approaching this zone of mental death; within a millionth of a second he would be within it—

Lux reached out with a surge of frantic speed, deflecting the mind-killing field, bending it aside—

And sagged, panting at the closeness of his escape.

Had his sensories not been extended to scrutinize the anti-gravitic field, even his automatic survival mechanism could hardly have detected the death zone in time, for the heterodyning field was a mere trickle of low energy, so faint are the electrical impulses of human thought-waves.

His mind would simply have been helpless, and for all his superhuman powers, he would have been dysfunctional. Death would have followed instants later with the failure of the unconscious nervous system, which controls the circulation of blood, the heartbeat, and the operation of the lungs.

With a blinding flash of intuition, it came to him then that this automatic death zone shielded the living quarters of Malaire from any unwarranted intrusion.

Doubtless, assassination was a lost art in this century of the Urban Age. The citizens of Arthex were too weak, too drunk on sensuous pleasures, too essentially frivolous to conceive or undertake a political murder. The intellectual cadre that surrounded the City Master, however, might well contain one or two individuals capable of ambition, hungry to dislodge Malaire and to seize control of the pinnacle of power he inhabited.

The death zone effectively sealed him off from any potential assassin, even a sentient machine such as one of the robot guards. They, too, would be wholly vulnerable to the field of mind-disrupting force.

Probably, very few of them were ever admitted into the actual presence of Malaire. And those few would have to be provided with some insulation or protective defense against the death zone.

It came to him that this was the *insignia* to which the automaton had referred. He recalled the puzzling question the robot guard had directed to him during their brief conversation in the corridor beyond the examination room. He strove to recall the exact wording of the query—

"The private tube is waiting; you will, of course, have your insignia about your person."

At the time, uncertain as to what meaning the automaton had placed on the word "insignia," Lux had presumed the creature was asking about some sort of personal identification—some kind of credentials he might be called upon to display before being admitted into the presence of Malaire. Now he decided the robot had inquired about a protective device those summoned to the private suite of the City Master were required to have in their possession in order to pass safely through the mind-destroying zone of mental death.

Rapidly searching the pouchlike pockets of the

borrowed clothing he had donned in the examination room, Lux found a sort of brassard that had to be the insignia to which the automaton had referred.

It was an armlet of organic crystal unfamiliar to him. Lux studied its molecular structure swiftly, noting that the crystalline lattice contained a dormant pattern of weak electromagnetic force.

Had the brassard been energized, he decided, it would have surrounded him with a faint aura of electrical pulsations which would doubtless have nullified the energy flow of the death zone. Probably each member of the intellectual cadre which ruled or administered the Living City under the supreme authority of Malaire was required to bear this insignia upon his person at all times. It followed, then, in logical sequence, that only Malaire himself could energize the protective brassard—and would do so only when he desired a particular member of the cadre to report to him in person.

And Lux had unwittingly borrowed the clothing of one of the *other* technicians, not knowing that it was another of them whose brassard had been energized by remote control, and that he was going to certain death, bearing with him a useless insignia whose protective forces remained dormant and inoperative.

With a sigh of relief, Lux thanked his lucky stars that idle curiosity or mere whim had impelled him to study the anti-gravitic field with his energy-sensitive mental extensions precious moments before the stasis field had carried him into range or the mind-destroying barrier!

This system of protective brassards must be the reason why Lis and Havering had required a neuro-radionic superman to penetrate the fastnesses of Central. If it had not been for the mind barrier, surely Havering could have found his way into Malaire's suite and either assassinated the despot or forced him at gunpoint to shut down the Null Sphere, permitting the ravening energy beams of the Weapon

Machine to destroy the defenses of Arthex.

But the death zone surrounding Malaire's eyrie made it impossible for any assassin to enter his presence. Only those of the ruling cadre he desired to admit to his offices for a personal interview could safely pass through the zone of mind-destroying force, and undoubtedly they were carefully screened.

But a superman able to manipulate, counteract, or even utilize energy barriers of any kind could penetrate any barrier. The test, of course, had been Lux's ability to safely pass through the Null Sphere itself. He now realized this, and simultaneously two other thoughts occurred to him in rapid sequence.

The first of these was that the controls of the Null Sphere must be situated somewhere in Malaire's private suite. For if they were located anywhere else in the Living City, there would be no reason why the silver-haired sage could not reach and deactivate them. For surely only Malaire's suite would be shielded by the mind-destroying zone of force.

Lux felt a heightened sensation of excitement. Within mere moments he would have penetrated into the inner adytum of the City. Its Master would be in his power, and in his power, as well, would be the goal and object of all his perils, adventures, and traveling. For, with Malaire helpless, he could switch off the Null Sphere, end the stifling Urban Age, and liberate the sorry remnants of mankind from their self-imposed imprisonment.

He could set man free!

But simultaneously with this revelation, a second thought came to him.

Havering and Lis were both able to travel through time. This had been amply demonstrated, as both of them had appeared to him physically in his own remote century. They could move through time and space with ease—they, too, were able to penetrate the Null Sphere, for he had seen both of them within the city of Arthex—and this presented a new dimension to the mystery of their true motives.

For if one possesses the power to move freely through

time, one can move with equal freedom through space itself,

For there cannot possibly exist any barrier that is impenetrable to a time-traveler. No matter how destructive a barrier may be, a time-traveler can find its spatial location, enter that point in an age before the barrier existed, *and travel into the future, appearing behind the barrier with perfect ease.*

If that was true, as simple logic told him, then Lis or Havering could have bearded Malaire in his den any time they wished!

But they had not done so; instead, they had taken him from his own remote century and brought him into the future to do the task for them.

Why?

He puzzled over this, frowning.

Unless they had lied to him about their ultimate purpose—unless they actually *did not* want the Null Sphere removed, the Living City destroyed, and the human race set free—their failure to act was completely inexplicable.

He was convinced that, from whatever motive, they did indeed work for the destruction of Arthex. Everything that had happened up to now hinged upon that fact. True, they both seemed to be his enemies, from some secret motive he could not understand, but he was convinced, nevertheless, that they did indeed desire the destruction of the Living City and the liberation of the race. If this was *not* so, their words and actions were nonsensical!

Lux felt a growing inner excitement.

It was as if his mind was a caged bird that had buffeted with beating wings against the bars of that cage. *And those bars were beginning to give way!*

He was very close to the ultimate answer, and he knew it.

The secret meaning of all the puzzling things that had been happening to him was almost within his grasp.

With inhuman speed, his augmented mind sorted through facts and theories, approaching the ultimate core—the reality behind the mask of mystery the Arcadians had drawn between him and everything that had yet happened to him since the moment the pistol had appeared in his office, aimed at his brow.

He began to see the outlines of the truth at last.

Almost everything that had been said to him was true—*almost!*

But almost everything that had *happened* to him was false—or had been cunningly designed, by those master psychologists of the distant Arcadian Age, in such a manner that he would derive a false picture of events from their sequence.

Almost!

And now he knew the truth at last.

His eyes widened with amazement; his lips pursed in a soundless whistle of surprise.

The implications of his discovery unfolded before him, one by one.

And they were—*incredible!*

Lis, he now realized, had never appeared to him physically at all. Her seeming materializations had been only an illusion.

It was impossible for intelligent beings to physically travel through time.

He quickly amended that, for an exception occured to him: the Weapon Machine, an artificial intelligence, had traveled back from the Arcadian Age to the present era.

A machine, then, even one that possessed sentience, could time-travel. *But humans could not!*

Why this was an impossibility remained uncertain to him. Perhaps the molecular composition of their bodies was inextricably part of the total entropic structure of any given period of time. In this connection, he recalled the amazement of the Arthesian technicians when they had discovered his own bodily entropy belonged to an earlier era.

Perhaps the mental pattern of a living human mind was woven into the energy structure of the age into which it was born; part of the total energy equation of total mankind in its native era, the human brain could not extricate itself.

Perhaps. It really did not matter.

What mattered was that he alone could move freely through time. Because he did not move *through* it, any more than he had moved through the Null Sphere. To move *through* time—to force the energy structure of a human mind either up or down the flow of time—might be to destroy it, to erode the lines of force that were the patterns of memory, the mental system that comprised an individual man.

Just as he had bent space, teleporting himself from one point in space to another *without actually traversing the intervening spatial distance between the two points*—so also did he "bend time."

He alone had the power to teleport through time. Or space, as far as that mattered.

Lis, then, was a resident of the remote future, and all she had projected back into his age, or into this age, was an illusion of her physical presence.

This *must* be true! He recalled that he had never touched her. When she had given him the little metal tube she claimed could rescue him from a hopeless trap, she had not handed it to him—*but tossed it through the air.*

She had not been physically present there in his bedroom at Havering's house in the twentieth century; being a living human being, she could not be. Only an illusion of her, artificially stimulated within his own brain. Lux recalled reading of experiments on the nerve centers of the brain: a weak electrical charge induced visual hallucinations when directed into the visual centers of the brain; aural or tactile or even olfactory hallucinations could also be generated if the stimulus was applied to those centers.

Obviously, then, immaterial forces had been aimed at his brain centers from the future, generating complex illusions of reality.

The tube itself, which she had seemed to toss

through the air for him to catch, was the only thing physically present in the room. Whatever that small instrument had been, it was merely a machine and could be thrust physically back through time, even as the gigantic Weapon Machine had been.

What about Havering/Sonthus?

Lux decided he must be a resident of this portion of the Urban Age. The person Lux had known as Jonas Havering in the twentieth century was another mentally induced illusion. In this case, Havering was as helpless a prisoner here in the Urban Age as the Lady Lis was in her own Arcadian epoch. Lux had been artificially induced to believe he had known Havering for many years. This must not have been particularly difficult for the master psychologists of Arcadia. If they could feed stimuli into his brain centers, convincing him that he was seeing and hearing a physically present human being where there was nothing but empty air, surely they could imprint false memories in his cortex, convincing him that for many years he had known a man named Havering.

Once this essential fact was realized, much that had been mysterious fell into place.

The pistol that had fired on him from empty air—the driverless car that had run him down without a hand at the wheel—were also mere machines. Either they had been manipulated by immaterial energies projected from the future—which was completely possible—or they too, like the simulacra of Lis and Havering, had been mere complex sensory hallucinations. Whichever they were was of no real importance: what mattered was that he realized at last why the two murder attempts had been seemingly supernatural.

One mystery, however, was left unexplained, and that was—why had his enemies tried to destroy him?

Smiling, Lux realized he had an answer to that one, too.

It was the simplest answer of all.

They had NOT.

XII. *The Metal Brain*

JOHN LUX had been so busy with these lines of thought that he had almost lost touch with his physical surroundings. Now he became aware that his flight up the transparent cylinder was slowing to a halt. A panel opened before him; he stepped from the shaft into a luxurious foyer. His feet sank into lush carpeting; the City Master, it seemed, preferred something a bit less utilitarian as his floor covering. No resilient plastic for the enigmatic Malaire!

The foyer was sourcelessly illuminated with a soft golden glow. Precious metals glistened about the foyer, the luster of pure gold, the sheen of silver, the dull glisten of platinum. Gems flashed in abundance. It was like the entrance way to a palace, Lux thought amusedly.

He crossed the thick carpets to a tall portal sheathed in plates of gold, opulently sculptured and studded with flashing gems. The door swung open soundlessly at his approach.

He found himself standing on the threshold of a room of breathtaking magnificence.

The domed ceiling, far above his head, was an enormous expanse of stained glass, radiant with a hundred jewel-bright hues. Statues of ivory, alabaster, rare marble, scented fruitwoods, ebony, and less familiar substances that were probably synthetics stood about the huge room on pedestals or ensconced in wall niches.

The walls were hung with gorgeous tapestries; curious three-dimensional paintings that flickered with movement as if they were pseudo-alive portraits or mobile tableaus hung between superb columns of carved stone. Scattered about the room, hand-crafted furniture culled from various epochs were carefully positioned. The entire room was redolent of palatial luxury, even of magnificence.

And the entire room centered about a single man.

Every line and curve, every vista and surface, led the eye to his face.

It was a powerful face, as if a sculptor of supreme genius had been asked to design features that spoke to the eye of those talents mankind desires in its ultimate and absolute leaders. Lux sensed a rigid self-control in the set of the broad, sloping shoulders, in the position of the relaxed, half-folded hands. There was an almost regal pride in the lofty poise of the head; willpower was visible in the square jaw and the modeling of the mouth; a vast, cool intelligence burned in the depths of dark, thoughtful eyes, deep and wide-set under the polished dome of a broad, high forehead.

It was Malaire, Lord of Arthex, despotic ruler of mankind; it could be no other.

He sat before a vast and empty desk, a glittering expanse of waxed mahogany. He was neatly and quietly dressed in a dark suit of some rich, expensive material, superbly tailored to hug the lines of his powerful body. Even in repose, he radiated an aura of power, of masculinity, of command, that was all but tangible.

Here, you felt even at the first glance, was a superman born to control the destinies of millions. Your eye was caught by the forceful molding of his face, held by the magnetism of his dark, brooding, intense gaze. The charisma you sensed about the seated—about the virtually *enthroned*—figure was, you guessed, the same radiant and magnetic force that, over the long ages of the past, had drawn men to serve similar supermen: Alexander, Caesar, Napoleon, Hitler.

The lure of those eyes was compelling—almost hypnotic.

It *was* hypnotic!

His senses stirring with a faint premonition of alarm, John Lux tore his eyes from that magnetic gaze.

In the next instant, deadly forces shimmered around him. An ordinary human being would have died in split seconds under that complex bombardment of energies that flickered up and down the scale of the electromagnetic spectrum. But John Lux diverted them, or canceled them out. Then he extended his sensories—traced the deadly flow of forces to hidden instrumentation in the walls, concealed behind glorious hangings—and rendered those power sources harmless.

To do so, he was required to nullify all electromagnetic force in the immediate area.

The powerful body slumped forward bonelessly across the glistening, empty expanse of the desk. The kingly brow nodded—drooped—fell on the folded hands.

Alarm—and a vague sense of intuition—flashed through Lux. He probed out, searching with delicate, energy-sensitive tendrils of thought the slouched, unmoving figure of the City Master.

And found it was not alive.

Was not even—*human!*

It took the neuro-radionic superman mere moments to penetrate to the heart of yet another mystery.

The enormously vital, powerful, impressive figure of Malaire was a synthetic thing, human-looking only to the exterior gaze. To the sensory perception of John Lux's enormously evolved nervous system it became immediately obvious that what the world of this age believed to be the omnipotent dictator Malaire was only a flesh robot.

A superficial exploration of the entire suite consumed a few more minutes, but offered definite proof that no such person as Malaire existed.

For the remainder of the apartments reserved for the Master of the Urban Age were completely empty and untenanted. The rooms that should have been palatial dining rooms, bedrooms, sitting rooms, and bath facilities were completely devoid of furnishings and decorations.

Save for the sumptuously appointed audience hall, the suite of Earth's master was—empty!

A few more moments of search confirmed Lux's discoveries. Malaire was a mere simulacrum, a clever imitation of synthetic flesh, filled with ingenious mechanisms to simulate human expressions, voice intonations, gestures.

The control elements were set into the frame of the thronelike chair in which the flesh robot had been seated when Lux had canceled out all energy flows in the immediate vicinity in order to call a halt to the bombardment of forces that had been directed against him.

His sensories probed into the structure of the chair; as he suspected, they were directly linked to the City Brain—the unthinkably vast supercomputer that ran the entirety of the Living City.

In a moment of swift thought, John Lux reached a decision on the course of action he would next initiate.

He lugged the flesh robot from the chair, depositing it on a satin-covered divan some yards away.

And seated himself in the control chair, in Malaire's place—

and found himself plunged into multi-level contact with the *real* Master of Arthex!

The artificial intelligence was vast and cool and awesomely complex, and so ancient that probably no sentient thing in the unending reach of eternal time had ever approximated its enormous age.

For more than ten thousand years—Lux did not then ascertain the precise period at which the Living City had been constructed—it had monitored the tremendous life-support system that men called Arthex.

Self-repairing, self-powered, the colossal City Brain yet lacked self-initiative. Far from being a sinister computer-gone-mad, it was as selfless as any other tool.

Men had designed it to cope with a vast range of problems. Men had supplied it with the means to perpetuate itself. Remote-controlled bore-vessels searched out hidden veins of ore far beneath the Earth's crust; completely automatic factories turned raw ore into machinery. Robotic hydroponic farms in subterranean caverns provided the foodstuffs, the liquors, the pharmaceutical products whereby the Living City maintained its structure and nurtured its captive populace.

Men had built it to house and shelter and protect the survivors of the planet-devastating City Wars that had laid civilization in ruins and transformed the world into a hostile and savage wilderness. Today, more than ten thousand years later, the gigantic machine was still doing so.

It would do so forever.

When threatened, the City Brain defended itself.

When the Arcadians had launched the Weapon Machine against Arthex, the City Brain had analyzed the problem, had measured the relative success-potential of a number of alternative plans of defense, had tapped the vast technological resources of its memory banks, and had erected the Null Sphere.

That had happened a thousand centuries ago.

The Weapon Machine still hovered above the City, still ravening for its destruction. Thus the City Brain continued to maintain the Null Sphere; it would maintain it indefinitely, for as long as the presence of the Weapon Machine made the existence of the Null Sphere a necessity.

It would maintain it forever.

Lux probed further, searching more deeply into the memory banks, uncovering more data.

The City Brain was not cognizant of the passage of time. That is, it recorded the passing years on a statistical basis, but had no conception of time as an essential factor. It knew that men were born, lived, and died under its protection. But this was a natural thing, a fact. The Brain drew no conclusions from that fact.

It was not aware that the human race was dying

out, smothered by the all-enveloping protectiveness of the Living City.

Or, rather, it was aware of the declining birthrate, but drew no conclusions from the fact that the number of births was shrinking from century to century. The fact was a statistic; a statistic to be recorded and forgotten; merely a numerical factor of relevance to food production, housing, and environmental maintenance.

In the essential meaning of the word, the City Brain could not really *think*.

Lux dug deeper, intrigued.

Malaire was a nonentity, a spokesman through which the City Brain maintained its basic communication with its charges. He was a figurehead, a mere symbol to which the administrative cadre and technical personnel could relate on the human level.

It was no wonder that his origin remained an enigma even to the Arcadians of the future. It was not surprising that they speculated as to the mystery of his past, wondering if he might not be an immortal.

Since Malaire did not really exist and never had, he could not be and was not John Lux's enemy.

Neither was the City Brain itself. It was not capable of emotion; it could not be vindictive.

The City Brain had not sent the Silver Men into the past to hunt him.

Lux tensed with amazement, and dug deeper:

The memory banks did not contain any knowledge of the Silver Men at all!

The Lady Lis, it would seem, had lied about this matter. But why? What could she gain from confusing him on the point of their origin?

One conclusion was obvious. If it was not Malaire —not the artificial intelligence that was the Living City of Arthex—which had directed the Silver Men to hunt him down, it could only be Lis herself. Lis, or Havering; the master psychologists of the Arcadian Age, whoever they were those faceless superintellectual strategists of the distant future, had been the only force opposed to him. Lux explored the memory banks of the City Brain, and found no evidence to the contrary.

The City Brain knew nothing of his existence in the twentieth century, and had no record of a neuro-radionic superman having ever been born. Its records, in fact, did not even stretch back to his own age.

It had not been Arthex that had directed those attempts to kill him.

It had been—Arcadia.

Lux had already reached the tentative conclusion that the attempts to kill him back in his own century had, in fact, been illusions—manufactured hallucinations, designed by master psychologists to motivate him along certain directions, and to impel him into certain courses of action.

Hence his discovery that it had not been the Living City from which the illusions had been projected fitted his first conclusions. Now he confronted the question of why these things had been done.

Withdrawing his tendrils of mental force from the memory banks of the City Brain, Lux broke the connection and began to think things out. His tentative conclusions thus far went in this manner:

1. *The Arcadians had attempted to persuade him to believe that his life was endangered by the Living City.*
2. *It was quite likely, however, that his life had not been in danger at all.*
3. *The attempts on his life had been nothing more than complex visual, aural, and olfactory illusions.*

Thinking back over the incidents, it occurred to John Lux that the only method of computing the hidden motive behind this tissue of lies and illusions was to consider exactly what they *had* accomplished.

The gun that had seemed to fire upon him—the

driverless car that had seemed about to run him down—what had those twin illusions actually resulted in?

The answer, when it came, was both utterly simple and completely obvious.

They had made him teleport.

The ability to teleport was only one factor in his neuro-radionic powers. But it was a dramatic factor.

His powers had lain dormant within him throughout his entire lifetime. Only once before, that time in Korea, when his life had been endangered, had his automatic survival mechanism been forced to tap his neuro-radionic powers in order to teleport him to safety.

Therefore, the illusory attacks, which had *seemed* to place him in a position of danger as hopeless as his position had been years before in that doomed tank, must have been—*could only have been*—designed to make him teleport again!

The motive behind the pretended murder attempts was explicable only by the result they had directly caused.

The Arcadians had wished him to realize that he possessed the ability to teleport. One such inexplicable, almost supernatural experience in a man's life can perhaps be passed off as a curious event. It can be forgotten, as the mind tends to forget things it does not want to remember, and things it cannot explain. *Just as he had in fact forgotten all about it, until Havering had reminded him of the odd event in his past!*

Very well, then.

But again—*WHY?*

There were probably several reasons. For one thing, to limber up his dormant faculty, as one exercises an unused muscle one is going to need.

For another thing, to drive the fact home to his conscious mind that he could indeed teleport when he had to.

But, he realized, it was not so much his ability to teleport himself through space that was so important to the mysterious masterminds of the Arcadian Age. *The REALLY important thing was his ability to teleport himself through time.*

For Lis or Havering could project an image of themselves through space and time, but only John Lux could transport his physical body. He could go where they could not go—or, rather, where a mental illusion was of no value whatsoever. For their presence in his own age, he now felt certain, had been a hallucination artificially suggested to his mind by the master psychologists of distant Arcadia.

In effect, they had hypnotized him.

But a *machine* cannot be hypnotized.

There could be no question but that the City Brain could protect itself from outside influence. Its sensory mechanisms must be insulated against any such outside tampering, even against an energy flow directed at it from the depths of the future.

Only the neuro-radionic superman could command energy, could extend tendrils of thought into the memory banks of the cold, soulless metal brain that was the Living City.

In fact, as he had done so, John Lux had been aware of protective devices within the City Brain being triggered into action by the fact of his mental intrusion. But, being John Lux, he had nullified or disarmed these protective mechanisms almost without effort.

His conclusions, then, were that the illusory attacks upon his life had served a double purpose. On the one hand, they had convinced him that Malaire mercilessly sought to destroy him; on the other, that he was a neuro-radionic superman.

Knowing that you possess a talent is half the battle in mastering it.

The first two attacks had thrust him into flight, had brought him to Havering's house, where a carefully contrived conversation subtly reminded him of his prior use of his teleportational powers, thus setting the stage for the appearance of the Lady Lis, who had given him a story neatly compounded of truth and untruth.

Following her advice, he had flown to Weston.

Then the master psychologists of Arcadia had projected the illusion of the Silver Men . . .

But—wait a minute! *Had* they been an illusion? Hadn't one of them blasted the engine of his plane, forcing him down in a crash landing? And hadn't they set the forest afire to smoke him out?

Had they? He recalled that while he had seen the light of the forest fire, he had smelled no smoke—*even though the wind had been blowing in his direction*. Even at the time, harried and hunted and goaded to desperation, he had noticed his inability to smell the smoke. At the time, he had been so busy escaping with his life that he had merely observed and mechanically stored away the fact, too busy to think about it.

But an olfactory illusion must be a very difficult illusion to maintain. Probably the nerve connections are more subtle than in mere vision. The eye can be very easily fooled by the simplest bit of trick photography, the easiest item of make-up or disguise, the most rudimentary optical piece of trickery. The eye, in fact, fools itself into seeing what it is told or suggested that it is seeing—as every stage magician knows!

But it is very difficult to fool your sense of smell. The one and only time any segment of the sequence of illusions had been accompanied by an olfactory hallucination, rather than merely by visual or aural effects, had been that of the revolver that had fired at him. He could vividly recall the metallic stench of cordite in his office. The illusion of the smell of gunpowder must have been an extremely difficult one to produce—*too* difficult to repeat!

But what about the engine of his aircraft? He remembered that gout of blue-white fire the Silver Man had directed into the cowling of the motor from outstretched fingertips. How can a visual hallucination stop a plane dead in mid-air?

Lux shrugged; perhaps the engine had stalled when he had instinctively jerked back the controls . . . or perhaps an energy flow had been timed to coincide

with the visual effect of the destructive burst of fire
. . . it did not really matter which was the answer.
The fact remained the same. Even the Silver Men
had been empty illusions . . .

Designed to produce what result?

His mind hovered on the edges of the ultimate discovery, when a flicker of unexpected movement at
the edge of his vision distracted his attention from
his thoughts. He looked up.

*And there stood Lis and Havering, smiling at him
gravely.*

XIII. *The Weapon Machine*

JOHN LUX struggled to retain a calm, impassive demeanor before the two Arcadians who had tricked and bedeviled him with lies and illusions for so long.

For a moment he remained silent, studying them curiously. Their appearance here at this time could have only one implication: time was running out, and the Crisis Point was almost upon them.

In mere moments, he might be called upon to make a decision of incalculable importance. A decision that would affect the future history of human civilization. *A decision, moreover, that he alone could make.*

For a moment he yielded to an all-too-human weakness, wishing that a decision of such enormity could have been passed into other, more capable hands. Then this moment of vacillation passed; he felt new determination welling up within him, a readiness to accept and to face up to the role of transcendant importance that history had thrust upon him.

For, just as he was the only human being who possessed the power to destroy the Null Sphere, so was he the only human being able to decide whether or not it *should* be destroyed.

The Arcadians had melted into being out of empty air, and they were just as he had last seen them. Lis, her tall, lithe figure attractively clad in some tight-fitting dark stuff that caught the light and glittered intriguingly as she moved; Sonthus in his severe gray raiment, his make-up discarded now that it was no longer needed, his features those of Lux's old friend, Jonas Havering.

The Arcadians were silent, waiting for him to speak. He surveyed them thoughtfully but said nothing, busied with his own thoughts and with the momentous decision he soon would have to make.

The Lady Lis glanced with poorly concealed impatience at a small instrument like a wristwatch which somehow adhered directly to the flesh of her wrist, not requiring a strap.

"Time is fast running out, John Lux!" she said rapidly. "The ultimate Crisis Point has almost come. According to our estimate, you should by now be in possession of all the facts. Why, then, do you hesitate?"

"I am in possession of *almost* all of them," Lux corrected her gently. "One or two points still await clarification."

Her lovely eyes flashed.

"Then ask your questions, if you must—but swiftly! There is so little time until—"

Jonas Havering interrupted her outburst of impatience suavely.

"Just a moment, my dear. John Lux, let us discuss where we stand at the brink of this cataclysmic decision. Correct me if I am wrong, but obviously you have mastered your neuro-radionic powers and can control them with your conscious mind. Am I correct?"

Lux nodded calmly.

"Yes, of course," he said. "Without having achieved conscious mastery of my power to manipulate, divert, or control all forms of energy, it would not have been possible for me to have escaped from your aircar and from the energy trap you had devised for me. Incidentally, am I correct in assuming that the energy trap was a very real danger? I suspect, in fact, that it represented the only genuine peril I have yet faced in the course of these adventures."

Havering smiled approvingly.

"Very good, John Lux! I see our faith in you was not in the least degree misplaced. Yes, the energy trap was genuine and would have destroyed you had you not gained conscious control of your powers in time to escape from it. But your life was also in very real danger during that automobile accident on the bridge, when you lost control of your vehicle and it plunged through the rail into the river. That was quite real too; however, it was purely accidental, and not due to our planning at all. *Real* accidents do happen, even to neuro-radionic supermen, as you know, of course. You will have decided by now that the previous attempts on your life were nothing more dangerous than extremely complex sensory hallucinations, induced by energy flows directed at the nerve centers of your brain by the master psychologists of Arcadia in the distant future. The energy trap, however, was very real, and would have destroyed you had you not gained that conscious control of your powers—which has all along been the motive hidden behind our various actions against you. What else have you learned?"

In a quiet, musing voice, Lux recited his discoveries concerning the illusory presence of Havering and the Lady Lis, and the true nature of Malaire, the City Brain, and the Living City itself.

"There is, however, one other detail which continues to baffle me," he concluded. "And that is the nature of the small metal tube which the Lady Lis gave me back in the twentieth century, saying it would take me to a place of safety if ever I became hopelessly trapped. I became so trapped when my car went over the bridge, and I used the tube as she had directed me when the car was sinking under the river and I could not get out—"

Havering nodded.

"But the tube did nothing when I used it!" Lux said. "I teleported through time myself, I am convinced of it!"

Again, Havering nodded.

"Quite correct," he agreed. "The ability to time-port is one of your intrinsic powers as a neuro-radionic superman. But you must pause to reevaluate the situation for just a moment. The seeming attacks on your life, up to that point, had been devised in part to convince your conscious, reasoning mind that you could in fact teleport from a dangerous, a potentially lethal, situation. It was a far more difficult task to convince you of your ability to move through time. Granted, the metallic tube given to you by the Lady Lis was merely an instrument which contained a high-speed sound recording, and not a machine capable of extricating you from your difficulties; still and all, the tube *did* extricate you!"

"What was the message contained in the tube? I was conscious only of a jabbering noise—"

"The verbal message was played at high speed," Havering said. "Your conscious mind could make nothing of it, but we were attempting to bypass your conscious mind and to communicate directly to your subconscious mental processes, then still in solitary command of your neuro-radionic powers, including your abilities to teleport and especially to timeport. There was, you see, not time enough to attempt to convince your logical, reasoning mind that you could timeport. But your subconscious mind is not governed by logic or reason; it is a primitive thing of pure instinct. And it is that layer of your mind that contains a complete sensory recording of every moment of your bodily life. The subconscious, you know, remembers every sound and sight, every taste and touch and odor you have ever experienced, including all those your concious mind has forgotten."

"I don't quite understand," Lux confessed.

"To your conscious mind, the chittering squeal of noise given off by the metallic tube was a meaningless jabber. But your subconscious recorded it, as it records every sense impression, and could in effect 'play it back' by slowing it down. The message simply said that you could teleport through time, and delivered to your subconscious the space/time coordinates to which we desired you to teleport."

"But I don't see how—"

"Your concious mind would pause to doubt, to consider, to question," Havering declared. "Your blind, instinctive subconscious merely acts. It acted—and you teleported. Not quite to the correct spatial position, but close enough to make only a little difference."

Lux was astounded at the simplicity of the deception.

"And that's *all?*" he demanded incredulously "The tube did nothing more? Just told me I could teleport, and gave me the when and where to which I *should* teleport?"

Havering smiled.

"That's all; nothing more," he confessed. "Oh, the molecular structure of the metal composition of the tube was also entropically keyed to the precise entropy level of this portion of the Urban Age, so that once you had freed yourself from the central time-track it 'pulled' in the direction of its proper place in the entropic spectrum of eternity. That was merely an additional safety factor, though."

Lis was looking at the chronometer she wore on her wrist. The impatience and desperation she felt were audible in her harsh, strained voice and her white, tense features.

"We have no further time to squander on fruitless explanations," she said, breaking in on the conversation. "The Crisis Point is only twenty-four minutes in the future. You must destroy the Null Sphere *now*, John Lux!"

He regarded the handsome young woman meditatively.

"What happens if I do not destroy it at just the correct time?" he inquired curiously.

"But you must!" she cried. "Because you *did*—that is, the history of the Arcadian Age records the precise moment in time when the neuro-radionic superman from the past acted to break down the Null Sphere, thus precipitating the destruction of the Living City of Arthex—"

"And if I don't do it right on time, then what?" he asked.

Havering broke in, his eyes brooding and troubled.

"Just a moment, my dear," he said. "John Lux—*do*

you know how to destroy the Null Sphere? Please do not be hasty in making your reply; this is a very important question, and much hangs on the element of factual truth in your answer to it. Are you completely certain of your ability to destroy the Sphere?"

Lux stared at him musingly for a moment.

"Yes," he said truthfully. "I can destroy the Null Sphere at any time."

"Then am I not also correct in assuming that you can also destroy the Living City itself, should you so desire?" Havering pressed.

Lux was puzzled at the note of strain and urgency he detected in the other's tones; but he replied no less truthfully.

"I can."

"Very well, then! And are you not convinced that mankind must be liberated from this playground-prison if it is not to dwindle and die out?"

"Yes," Lux answered slowly, "I have become convinced of that as well."

At this point the voice of the Lady Lis broke impatiently into Havering's interrogation of Lux.

"Why, then, do you hesitate to do so?" she urged. "Why do you delay, John Lux, when every moment counts?"

"Because one element in this situation remains elusive," he replied frankly. "I have not yet come into any contact with the Weapon Machine itself. I have yet to ascertain its motives and intentions—"

"The Weapon Machine?" she demanded incredulously. "What of the Weapon Machine? Its only purpose is to destroy the Living City and liberate the human race into the wilderness. Surely you do not doubt this fact!"

"Not exactly *doubt*," replied Lux thoughtfully. "I do, however, wonder if the Weapon Machine will stop with the destruction of Arthex. What is to prevent it from slaughtering the inhabitants of the City during that destruction?"

The young woman looked nonplussed for a moment.

"But—it was carefully programmed by the master psychologists of Arcadia for that single purpose alone," she said. "It has been instructed in precise measures which will render the City inhabitable. It has been elaborately preconditioned to work no harm against the populace."

"Of course," Lux nodded. "But that conditioning was implanted in the memory cells of the Machine at least ten thousand years ago. How can we be certain the artificial mind of the enormous weapon from the future has not evolved the ability to reason for itself in all that time—how can we be sure that it has not developed new motivations of its own by now? You have admitted earier that Arcadia lost control of the Machine ages ago; how can we be positive the Machine is still obeying the instructions your Arcadian scientist instilled within it? Could it not by now have found a way to circumvent its own programming?"

A note of somber and thoughtful musing entered his voice.

"It remains a possibility that to destroy the Null Sphere and to render impotent the protective facilities of the City Brain might be to unleash upon the last helpless remnants of humanity in this age a ravening machine monster of destruction, whose programming has gone awry during the Ten-Thousand-Year Siege. The possibility is, I expect, a remote one; however, it remains a factor which I must evaluate before reaching my all-important decision."

"But the Crisis Point is almost upon us, John Lux!" the futurewoman cried desperately. "Further indecision on your part may throw into jeopardy the very existence of the future!"

"I am aware of that," he confessed in a troubled voice. "Yet the Weapon Machine has remained aloof throughout the course of this adventure. Not once has it made the slightest act of intervention in the flow of events. I have yet to confront it or to communicate with it, and while I have plumbed and discovered the ultimate realities behind Malaire and ascertained the true nature of the City Brain, I have as yet learned absolutely nothing concerning the inner workings of the sentient Machine. How can I take an act of such irrevocable finality without the slightest knowledge of the consequences? They might, indeed, prove ultimately disastrous—but I would find this out far too late to do anything about it. Why, for all I know, the instant the Null Sphere goes down, the Weapon Machine might totally vaporize all of Arthex with a nuclear-fission bomb. I *must* get in contact with the Machine before I take an act whose ultimate consequences I cannot foresee! Can you not understand this? Unleashing the Weapon Machine against the Living City might well prove to be the worst possible thing I can do!"

Her voice was raw with desperation.

"But there is *no time left,* John Lux! No time at all! The Crisis Point is now minutes away—you must reach your decision at once, and act upon it without further delay—or you will invalidate our history and throw the very existence of the future into peril. There is no time left for you to enter into communication with the Weapon Machine—no time at all!"

Lux tensed, aware that events were moving forward toward an unseeable, unguessable climax far too swiftly for his choosing. Logic and reason urged him to exercise caution in his next act; but the rapid movement of time itself gave him no leisure to contemplate the eventual outcome of the act, or the disastrous consequences that might result therefrom.

He became aware that he was being forced into taking an irrevocable act he might well bitterly regret. Suddenly, an iron stubborness—an unyielding determination—welled up in him. The master pshychologists of distant Arcadia had befooled and befuddled him ere this; he had had enough of being manipulated like a child, of being used like a mere tool. It was not at all impossible that this talk of the urgency and importance of the so-called Crisis Point was just another way of using him. He could not see why the Arcadians placed so much significance on the precise moment in time in which he must take the action they urged upon him. And he became convinced, in spite of the tension and note of naked desperation that lay behind the words of the futurewoman, that the urgency to act at a precise instant of time was not of the overriding importance she claimed it to be.

He was on the point of simply refusing to take any action before entering into communication with the Weapon Machine when a quiet voice interrupted his sequence of thought.

"You need not worry about establishing communications with the Weapon Machine, John Lux. For already you are in communication; know, John Lux, that *I am the Weapon Machine!*"

He turned in amazement to look upon the personage who had just made that astounding claim—

It was Jonas Havering!

XIV. *The Last Revelation*

JOHN LUX stared incredulously at Jonas Havering. Even the Lady Lis turned to regard her companion with amazement written in her expression.

As they watched, a strange transformation took place.

The human face is a shape of plastic flesh. Hundreds of tiny muscles behind that mask of flesh make it capable of a surprising number of contortions. It is this capacity to alter, this variety of flexible changes, that lends to the flesh mask what we call "expression."

In his entire life, John Lux had never seen a human face that was *completely* without expression.

He looked upon one now.

It was the face of Jonas Havering!

As he and the futurewoman watched, the vitality ebbed from the face, leaving it utterly devoid of expression, leaving it completely immobile. The utter serenity, the absolute calm, the machinelike quietude of those features lent the face of Jonas Havering an inhuman—or *superhuman*—impassivity.

All expression, all tone and intonation, had left the voice of Jonas Havering as well. When he spoke, it was with a mechanical tonelessness that stripped his words of all resemblance to the human voice. Once, Lux had attended experiments conducted with a voder—a clever device that imitates the human voice. Listening to that which had been Jonas Havering, Lux was reminded of that toneless, machine-perfect replication of human speech.

"Ten thousand years ago, when the Arcadian civilization sent me backward in time to this era and I

materialized in mid-air near the Living City of Arthex, I was automatically energized," said the voice
of the false Jonas Havering.

"During the first thirty-seven seconds after I had
become pseudo-alive, my reasoning centers scanned
and evaluated all relevant possibilities. Among these
was the inherent possibility that the City Brain
might erect some impassable barrier againt my energy weapons—a force wall which my armaments
would not be able to penetrate."

The serene features reflected no slightest shadow
of human emotion as the thing described its own
creation.

"With the enormous reserve facilities with which I
had been outfitted in order to ward against any emergency or situation that might arise, I constructed this
flesh robot and guided it into the Living City. To all
outward scrutiny, it was identical with a normal human being, and thus its appearance among the Arthesians occasioned no alarm or surprise. Indeed, no
one ever noticed the presence of a stranger in the Living City."

The flesh robot paused for an instant.

"I thus became a dual being," it continued.
"Shortly after my Machine-self commenced the bombardment of Arthex, the City Brain succeeded in
creating the impenetrable barrier you know as the
Null Sphere, which rendered further attempts by my
Machine-self to demolish the Living City futile. But
my Sonthus-self had already penetrated the inner
fastnesses of Arthex, and was free to attempt the destruction of the City from within its own defenses."

The flesh robot gestured at the Lady Lis.

"Thought alone is able to penetrate the Null
Sphere, as the energy waves of sentient thought do
not propagate in the medium of this continuum, but
in the sub-ether of an adjoining dimension of
space/time. Ere long the Arcadians discovered this as
well, and dispatched focused thought streams into
the City to investigate conditions within. The impasse created by the erecting of the Null Sphere was

soon discovered, and the master psychologists of the Arcadian Age strove to subvert the inhabitants of the City to their cause. My Sonthus-self became in time a seeming convert to the Arcadian cause; also in time, the Lady Lis was sent into the past to consult with me. I feel certain that she never once suspected that the philosophical revolutionary Sonthus was in reality little more than a clever approximation of a human being—a mere projection of the Weapon Machine itself."

"That is true," Lis whispered. "I never *dreamed*—"

The flesh robot observed her with its tranquil gaze.

"I did not deem it neccessary that you should know," the emotionless voice continued. Then, switching its gaze to Lux, the flesh robot continued its story.

"In time we discovered that a neuro-radionic superman had appeared at least once in human history, and together we conceived of our plan to awaken your dormant faculties—induce you to teleport into this age—guiding your every move to this very point of time. It is now within the reach of your powers to destroy the Null Sphere, to end the stalemate of the Ten-Thousand-Year Siege, and to free what remains of mankind from the stifling protectiveness of this closed environment."

The emotionless mask of what had been the face of Jonas Havering turned its serene and fathomless gaze upon him. And John Lux tensed, knowing that within mere seconds he would be forced to make the momentous decision he had delayed so long. Even more significantly, he would soon be forced to act upon that decision, and the results of that action, cataclysmic as they might well prove to be, were still unknown to him.

But again the flesh robot was speaking to him.

"In order to develop and train your superhuman powers, we have been forced to lie to you, to deceive you as regards many facets of the situation. We have even had to threaten you with seeming danger. For these deceptions, which were unfortunately quite necessary, we apologize. We did not enjoy lying to you or deceiving you, but these things had to be done in order for you to discover and develop the ability to control and command your own hidden potential."

Lux nodded.

"I understand; the dangers were no less fearful for being illusory, but I hold no hard feelings. What was done *had* to be done, and no one was hurt in consequence of them."

The flesh robot agreed quietly.

"Now we come to the final decision," it said. "There is only one way to convince you that the Weapon Machine does not secretly conspire to the destruction of the inhabitants of the Living City— that my Machine-self has not gone insane during the endless centuries of the Ten-Thousand-Year Siege. What I am about to do now will convince you beyond any other argument or proof I might offer. And I am only able to perform this act because I am confident of the truth of your statement . . ."

Lux frowned, puzzledly.

"What statement?"

"That it was within your power to destroy Arthex yourself," the robot said. "I am confident of the truth of that fact; otherwise I could not do what I must do next. Now listen to me closely, both of you . . ."

The homiform extension of the Weapon Machine strode across the room to the near wall, on which hung a gorgeous tapestry of many-colored metallic fabric, woven with exquisite artistry into a bewildering juxtaposition of interlocked geometric forms. Here the flesh robot paused, drawing the tapestry aside. An oval screen of ground glass was set into the wall behind the masking tapestry. Dials and tuning controls, set flush with the wall surface, were below the oval screen.

Manipulating the controls, the flesh robot attuned the vision screen. A brilliant glare lit up the opaque panel; it blurred with swirling colors, gradually sharpening into focus.

A vista of blue sky appeared. The ragged veils of grayish clouds drifted across the scene. Suddenly there loomed into sight a stupendous construction that John Lux recognized as the Weapon Machine itself. He started with surprise.

"How can this televisor operate?" he inquired sharply. "I should think it impossible for televisor waves to penetrate the impassable barrier of the Null Sphere."

The flesh robot nodded.

"Ordinarily, this would be so. But Malaire's private televisor does not operate on the same principles as a common set. This instrument is specially designed. It utilizes a unique spectrum of multiphasic light-waves which circumvent the continuum and thus pass unimpeded through the space occupied by the Null Sphere."

The robot fingered the controls with exquisite care. The picture sharpened its detail, drawing into careful focus. The precision with which the figure of Sonthus/Havering manipulated the controls of the televisor brought home to Lux once again the realization that the man-like figure before him was only a mechanism and not a man, however much it might resemble one.

"Observe," the flesh robot commanded them tranquilly.

Now they could see the Weapon Machine with superb clarity. Outside the black sphere that encompassed the City, it was a clear sunlit day. Every detail of the aerial construction was startingly vivid. The tremendous machine was shaped rather like a child's top, with the blunt end turned skyward and the pointed end toward the earth itself.

Weightless as a cloud, the tremendous mass of invulnerable metal floated above the Living City. All of bright scarlet metal was it made, and its surface was broken into a bewilderingly complex interplay of shapes. Rounded bosses and cubelike protuberances of unknown purpose thrust from it here and there; equally mysterious grilled or tubular orifices were visible at intervals about its circumference. A profusion of coiling tubes writhed about it, entering the surface to disappear within and emerging again at another point, seemingly at random.

Sunlight twinkled and glittered from the strange scarlet metal. Time did not seem to have marred the Weapon Machine in the slightest; ten thousand years of wind and weather had passed over the aerial metal monster without effecting the smallest visible change in its appearance.

John Lux stared upon it with fascination. It was weird to think that anything so huge, so immeasurably ancient, could be a sentient being, and stranger still to remember that it did not live for all that it could think. It was a lifeless thing of cold dead metal—inanimate, only a machine—yet it lived and thought and planned. And had fought the longest war in the entire record of human history.

The flesh robot turned to face them a last time. For a moment it observed them in silence, and in that instant it almost seemed to Lux that a shade of expressiveness crossed the perfect serenity of those immobile features. Was it the faint suggestion of emotion he glimpsed in that simulacrum of a human face?

Was it—loneliness?

Or even—sadness?

"Watch the televisor screen closely," the homiform figure bade them solemnly. "Soon you will understand why I do what I must do. Soon, John Lux, you will be able to reach your momentous decision with no shadow of doubt about the intentions of the Weapon Machine. And now—farewell to you both!"

And with those surprising words, the image of Jonas Havering—*vanished*.

The disappearance of Jonas Havering took both of them completely by surprise. The Lady Lis cried out in amazement, staring about her with wide, unbelieving eyes. Lux extended his sensories and scrutinized the emptiness of the room carefully; the energy flow which had sustained the illusion of Jonas Havering's presence in the room was no longer active. He exchanged a baffled glance with the young woman. Neither of them was able to guess what the curious action of the flesh robot might mean.

Then Lis gasped and pointed.

Lux turned to the brilliantly illuminated televisor. The screen revealed an astounding development.

For the first time in ten thousand years, the Weapon Machine began to move!

Whirling slowly on its axis, the flying island-fortress of blood-red metal began to rise into the atmosphere.

Farther and farther it lifted above the surface of the planet. Lux sprang to the controls, to change the setting of the dials in order to follow the flight of the Weapon Machine as it ascended. But this was not needed; it would seem the focusing mechanism of the televisor was already set to track any movement the gigantic Machine might make, for the viewpoint of the screen altered, following the ascent of the aerial construction of scarlet metal.

The televisor tracked it until it had ascended to the height of five miles. Beyond this point, seemingly, the televisor could no longer keep up with the skyward acceleration, for as it flew above the five-mile level, the image of the scarlet Machine dwindled visibly, becoming at length merely a minute fleck of bright metallic red against the darkening azure of the heavens.

"What is happening! Is the Weapon Machine abandoning the siege? I do not understand—nothing like this has ever happened before!"

There was amazement and alarm in the warm contralto voice of the futurewoman. Lux merely shrugged; he was unable to answer her query. This totally unexpected development had taken him by surprise, too, and he was as bewildered as she.

The Weapon Machine had now ascended to the height of ten miles above the planet.

At that moment the televisor rocked to a deafening concussion.

Intolerable light blazed against the dark heavens like the birth of a new star.

Sunlike, the globe of pure flame brightened fiercely.

The fireball expanded rapidly, losing its spherical shape, edges roughening.

From a globe of fierce, actinic whiteness, the expanding fireball yellowed—then reddened.

An enormous cloud of superheated gas and vaporized metal flowered in the upper reaches of earth's atmosphere.

The Weapon Machine was no more.

And gradually the meaning of this act of self-destruction began to dawn on John Lux.

As both the futurewoman from the Arcadian Age and the flesh robot of Jonas Havering had told him, time was running out. The Crisis Point was almost upon them. There was no time for leisurely argument, no time to offer Lux proof that would convince the man from the twentieth century that he could safely destroy the Null Sphere and permit the Weapon Machine to commence its long-delayed program of the destruction of the Living City.

So the Machine had, quite simply, destroyed itself.

Since it no longer existed, it could pose no potential menace to the surviving remnant of mankind who yet dwelled within the Living City.

Perhaps the Weapon Machine had already been mined with powerful explosive charges, and possessed the ability to self-destruct if it became necessary to do so. Or perhaps it had merely permitted its nuclear-fission engines to attain critical mass without automatically dampening the fission pile.

Whatever the method, it had destroyed itself—so that mankind might go free!

For a long moment, John Lux stared at the televisor screen with blank, unseeing gaze. An observer might have noticed a trace of moisture in his eyes. It might seem foolish to mourn a machine . . . a soulless, lifeless thing of inert metal. . . . a mere instrument, devised for a certain purpose by men, and superfluous once that purpose had been achieved.

But Lux was not thinking of the Weapon Machine as a vast, intricate aerial fortress that had stubbornly besieged the last redoubt of the human race for one hundred centuries.

He was thinking of Jonas Havering, thinking of the man who had once been his friend, and who no longer lived. He was remembering a warm, vibrant personality, a keen, alert intellect, a brilliant scholar, a fine human being. And, dwelling upon those memories, it made not the slightest importance to John Lux that the being he had called his friend was not a man, had never truly been a man, had in actuality only been a system of synthetic memories impressed upon the sensory receptors of his brain by energy flows directed from the distant future by a soulless mechanism . . .

A sharp cry woke him from his brief reverie.

The voice of the Lady Lis recalled him to the urgent reality about him. The Arcadian woman was staring at the odd chronometer she wore on her slender wrist. Tension and despair were visible in her distraught features.

She raised enormous dark eyes to his, eyes darkly shadowed with emotion.

"The time is . . . *now,* John Lux!" she cried.

"The Crisis Point?"

She nodded, dark hair tumbling about the pale oval of her tense face.

"*The Crisis Point is . . . NOW!*" she said.

XV. *The Crisis Point*

JOHN LUX sat himself swiftly in the huge, thronelike chair of Malaire's behind the vast, smooth desk of polished mahogany. The time for doubt and questioning was past; the moment of decision was upon him now, and he was swift to act.

The self-destruction of the Weapon Machine had decided him, just as the flesh robot who had once been Jonas Havering had known it would.

Rapidly, Lux put himself *en rapport* with the City Brain. The intricate mechanisms concealed in the great throne-chair were direct connective links with the hidden adyta of the metal mind that controlled the Living City. Now Jon Lux extended his sensories, infiltrating his mind extensions into the memory banks of the colossal artificial intelligence, as he had done earlier.

Automatic safeguards had been built into the throne receptors to prevent precisely this unwarranted intrusion; protective mechanisms that would have burned out the neuronic linkages of any lesser man.

But the neuro-radionic superman from the distant past was immune to any such attack. The hostile energy flows were diverted one by one, effortlessly turned aside, their mind-destroying forces harmlessly diverted.

With the very speed of thought itself, the sensory extensions of John Lux's remarkable mind traced a million miles of wiring to the central memory banks. Like a beam of light, his mind flashed through a billion connections to the ultimate center of being.

It was an eerie sensation, this mental penetration of another mind, and all the more uncanny in that the mind whose innermost recesses he was now probing was not even remotely human.

No warmth of simple, earthy emotion could be ascertained in the intricate play of cerebro-electrical impulses that flickered deep in the core of the City Brain. There was nothing here but a cold, eternal enormity of pure thought. John Lux lost all awareness of his own body, left behind in the great thronelike chair far above, in the uppermost tier of the central ziggurat of the Living City.

He now moved bodilessly through frigid darkness, at the ultimate center of the enormous artificial intelligence. He saw with senses other than sight, felt with senses subtler than touch. He was pure mind himself, here at the core of the mechanical brain, absorbed into the cold, flickering pulse of pure energy that moved through molecular patterns of steel and copper, crystal and plastic.

Electrons seethed about him, simultaneously tracing a billion predetermined paths between neuronic connections. To his bodiless gaze they were rapid pulsations of cold, violet light, moving through the synapses of a gigantic cortex.

The Brain itself was an enormous slab of synthetic plasticlike substance, built up of countless millions of transistors. Some of the memory paths were traced between the transistors themselves, but had this been true of the entirety of the City Brain, in order to maintain its many millions of simultaneous operations, it would have been larger than the City itself. No, the subtler memory complexes were paths linked between the very molecules of the plasticlike substance . . . layer on layer of molecular connections contained in the very crystal lattice of matter itself.

In utter darkness, in frigid sub-zero cold, the mind of John Lux penetrated into the innermost adyta of the City Brain, and entered into communication with it.

I sense the intrusion of an alien thought stream; what do you here, intruder?

The communication was purely mental, but to the sensory mechanism of John Lux's brain it was like a high, thin, singing voice. A voice as cold and thin and sharp as an arctic wind, blowing through needles of ice.

At the level of pure thought itself, John Lux replied to the query.

I have penetrated to this place to tell you that your mission is ended. The purpose for which you were designed and set in action no longer exists. Your further continuance is a negation of your own central directives. Your program is fulfilled.

Again, he received that cold, thin song of pure thought . . . the icy, mathematical music of naked electrons racing through frigid darkness.

So soon . . . so very soon? Is my cause for existence then at an end? Only ten millennia have passed since this most recent phase . . . only a hundred millennia since my systems were rendered operative . . . who shall guard and shelter mankind during all the many millions of years yet to come if I render myself de-energized?

Was it only his imagination, or did John Lux sense a note of melancholy, a whisper of sadness, in the cold music of the flickering electrons? He could not be certain; he never knew.

Henceforward, man shall take care of himself. It is now imperative that you render yourself inoperative. You have served your central directives well and faithfully and long, but they are now meaningless. It is time for you to rest.

Lux began to divert the internal energy flow within the City Brain.

Energy poured into empty, frigid blackness.

No longer did the cold purple fire of the electrons flash between the molecular lattices.

The Brain began to die . . .

Sector by sector, the tremendous slab of translucent synthetic went dark and cold. Light dimmed slowly through the vast and intricate works. The artificial intelligence weakened, its energy flows ebbed.

It sank slowly into an enormous silence.

But one last whisper echoed through the dying Brain . . . one final spasm of flickering electronic thought went flashing mournfully through the cold and empty darkness that closed down about the enormous sentience.

So soon . . . so soon? . . .

Then there was only the silence.

The silence that would never again be broken.

John Lux opened his eyes and found himself seated rigidly in the throne of Malaire. The Lady Lis was staring at him, her face white and strained, dark eyes enormous in the pallor of her features.

"The Crisis Point has . . . passed," she whispered.

He smiled somberly and a bit wearily.

"All is well," he said. "The Living City has been destroyed."

She regarded him with incredulity.

"Are you mad, John Lux, or do you jest?" she demanded. "The City stands yet!"

He nodded quietly.

"The City stands, yes, but it has fallen. Does that sound like a paradox?"

He rose from the throne chair and went in search of a window. He found sealed doors that gave forth on a small stone balcony; the doors had been sealed with a radio clock that opened only to the proper code signal on the proper wavelength. Now, of course, the lock was inoperable, and the doors swung open to the touch of his hand.

He led her forth on the balcony, and they stood looking down at the vista of the City.

For the first time in ages it lay open beneath blue skies. The black dome had ceased to exist. The cluster of artificial lights that had illumined the City like a gyre of captive suns had burned out; their brassy glare had given way to the rich flood of sunshine that now bathed the streets.

"But . . . what have you done?" she asked.

He grinned.

"It was not necessary to destroy the physical structure of Arthex in order to liberate mankind from this prison," he explained. "All that had to be done was to destroy the City Brain. Remember, Lis, that the Brain maintained everything in the entire City; with it now inoperable, *nothing in all of Arthex works any longer!"*

They looked down at the City. It was still a fantastic fairyland of quaint buildings, meandering streets, and endless amusements. But now, in the brilliant flood of sunlight, it seemed tawdry and garish, somehow.

And the City was truly dead. That could be seen at a glance. The aircars that had filled the skies of Arthex like a thousand glimmering soap bubbles now were fallen. The twinkling lights that had beckoned a childlike populace to an endless round of pleasures now had gone dark. In the streets far below they saw crowds of bemused Arthesians wandering aimlessly, puzzled by a catastrophe they could not begin to understand. Some stood about staring vacantly. Others lifted wondering eyes to a blue, cloud-flecked vault they had never seen before.

A fat woman, fantastically painted and bedizened, beat weak, pudgy fists futilely upon a wheelless carriage of blue plastic that would no longer hover weightlessly, nor carry her where she wished to go.

A young girl, her lithe, long-legged body naked save for designs of glittering paint, wrestled helplessly with the little glass doors of a public gustatorium. The girl was hungry, and tempting foods were before her, behind transparent panels. Always before those panels had sprung open to her touch; now they were fixed and immobile.

Still hungry, weeping with vexation, she wandered aimlessly away, seeking food elsewhere.

A stout and balding citizen, draped in maniacal scarlet robes, tugged and beat at the iris door of his residence. It would no longer open to admit him. It would never open again. The vast and intricate artificial intelligence that had powered the many millions of various devices and conveniences in the City was dead and lifeless.

At the edge of the City, where the warm, resilient pavement stopped abruptly, a horde of Arthesians had gathered, staring wonderingly out across the wilderness. Here there had been naught but the black, impassable barrier of the Null Sphere; it had been there longer than any of them could remember. Now the ebon barrier had vanished, and the people looked out on the surrounding wilderness whose very existence they had long since forgotten.

As the woman from the future and the man from the past watched, the first few Arthesians began to venture timidly out past the terminus of the City.

For the first time in ages, men of the Living City set foot upon the wilderness that was the earth.

Lis shivered suddenly.

"It is so sad," she said faintly. "They wander about, crying like frightened children, struggling with doors they cannot open, reaching for food they cannot take. How they will suffer in the years ahead!"

"Yes," he said. "It will be very hard for them. They will leave the City behind because it can serve them no longer. They will wander out into the barrens because there is no other place for them to go. They will suffer from hunger and thirst, from cold and from fear. Many of them will perish in the hostile wilderness—the timid, the weak, the frightened. Many will die. But some will live, will survive, will adapt. Some will find within themselves the courage and strength and endurance to wrest a meager living from the harsh soil of the wilderness. They will have to learn to hunt and kill, to plant grain and to cultivate the earth, to make fire and to find water. Those that do will become hardy and brave, and will father strong sons and fine daughters. They will rebuild civilization, but it will be a new kind of civilization, something never before seen on this ancient planet. They will not build cities, remembering how at the last their cities betrayed them and were found wanting. The lesson of Arthex they will never forget. Those who survive the grim trials ahead will be the founders of the Arcadian Age."

She turned away listlessly.

"So it is all over at last," she said. "Somehow I had expected something . . . *different*. But it *is* finished; the Crisis Point has come and gone; the survival of the future is now assured. My task here is ended. I can go home . . ."

"Yes," he smiled. "The past has lost, as it always loses; the future has won, as it always wins. How I wish I could see that 'brave new world' the survivors will someday build! Tell me, Lis, is marriage among the customs which will survive?"

His gaze was frank and candid. She flushed faintly before his gaze.

"Of course!" she said curtly.

"And, tell me then, are—*you*—married?" he asked.

"Why—" She bit her lip. "I am not yet wed," she replied.

"Nor am I," he admitted. "Lis . . . I would like to accompany you into the future. I would like to visit the world that I have helped to build. And I would like to know you better. All I have seen is an artificially induced illusion; I would like to get to know you in person . . . in the flesh, you might say!"

She drew herself up, primly.

"Need I remind you that, from my viewpoint, you are a barbarian—a mere savage?" she said, her voice freezing.

He was paying no attention to the tone of her voice. In fact, he seemed to be laughing at her. She flushed again, this time at the amusement in his eyes.

"Yes, I suppose I am," he grinned. "But you cannot convince me that women have changed *that* much in your century. A savage has certain things to offer that a very civilized man cannot!"

She tried to freeze him with an icy glare, but before the frank admiration in his eyes, her own gaze wavered and fell.

"I . . . I do not wish you to follow me," she said. "You must now return to your own time, and I to mine."

"Yes, but I don't need your permission to follow you into the future. Must I remind you that I have the power to teleport through time?"

Her eyes were angry. "And must *I* remind *you* of the limitations of your power? You cannot follow me to my native era because you do not know the year in which I live."

He grinned even more widely.

"Yes, but you could tell me the year, if you wished . . ." he said.

The young woman stiffened with reproof.

"I—" she began fiercely; then she broke off. And suddenly her figure began to fade from his vision.

But even as it did so, she suddenly raised her eyes to meet his gaze once more. And now she was smiling faintly, and there was a trace of warmth and humor in her eyes.

And—just before she vanished utterly—she leaned forward and recited a string of numerals.

Then she was gone from him.

Lux leaned against the balcony, grinning. The futurewoman from the Arcadian Age was surprisingly human, after all! That sequence of numbers represented the year in which she lived—the temporal coordinates at which he could find her, if he wished.

Did he wish? Well, why not? He could return to his own age at any time he wanted to; but there was little or nothing in the past to hold him now. The very thought of returning to his humdrum century was somehow wearisome; the vision of returning from this high adventure to take up the boring routines of business again was suddenly distasteful to him.

He remembered how she had looked—tall and lithe, her slim beauty gloved in glittering dark fabric. He dwelled on the pure oval of her face, on her lustrous dark eyes and sensitive, full-lipped mouth, and the dark splendor of her hair. He listened in his memory to the warm, vibrant contralto of her voice.

He had to admit that Lis excited him more than any woman he had known in his own century. Of course, nothing might come of their liaison; the gap between their cultures might well prove unbridgeable; her ultra-civilized way of life might prove distasteful to a mere savage such as himself . . . still and all, it was an intriguing adventure to contemplate.

And he was beginning to develop a taste for adventure.

He remembered the ice in her voice, and the stony glare of repulse in her eyes.

But there, at the very last, had there not been warmth and promise in the way she had told him her year?

"Well, what the hell—" said John Lux.

And the neuro-radionic superman from the twentieth century suddenly vanished, leaving the balcony empty. Below lay the dead metropolis and its dead past.

Ahead lay the unknown future. And no man can say what may happen—tomorrow.

One adventure had ended here on the stone balcony above the City.

But another adventure was just about to begin!

Author's Note

THIS BOOK is an affectionate tribute to one of the great masters of science fiction. Mr. A. E. van Vogt.

When A. E. van Vogt appeared on the scene, in the late 1930s, science fiction was undergoing its most important transition and was in the process of moving ahead, out of the Gernsbachian doldrums in which it had for too long been immured, into the Golden Age of John W. Campbell, Jr., and his great magazine, *Astounding Science Fiction*.

In the Campbellian revolution that was to re-shape science fiction into a mature and significant genre of popular literature, van Vogt was to play a leading role.

He sold his first story to a science fiction magazine in 1939. Almost from the first, he was recognized as a brilliant new talent. Before long, the pages of *Astounding Science Fiction* were filled with his stories. And they were great stories—stories like "Slan," and "The Weapon Makers," and "The World of Ā." Also before very long, the letter columns of *Astounding Science Fiction* rang with enthusiastic praise of his work. That clamor has never ceased, and A. E. van Vogt (yes, he *does* have a first name, but he dislikes it as much as I do my own) is still enormously popular, and still, I am happy to say, turning out marvelous stories.

Van Vogt pioneered a new kind of science fiction story: a style of story-telling with an intricate, convoluted plot which unraveled slowly, keeping the reader guessing and keeping him in suspense. I suppose the sort of intellectual puzzle-yarns van Vogt so ably spun are really more akin to the sort of locked-room mystery John Dickson Carr specializes in than to the ordinary run of science fiction. But they are science fiction nonetheless, and superbly entertaining.

When I was a young reader, devouring the pages of each issue of Campbell's *Astounding* with gusto and delight, van Vogt never failed to thrill me, to excite me. And now that I am a writer myself, I can appreciate from the technical end his marvelous facilities of plot and suspense. I have always wanted to try my own hand at a story of this type—a story in which the hero is a latent superman, being chased from pillar to post, helped and hindered or hunted by mysterious maybe-friends and equally enigmatic perhaps-enemies, struggling against time to learn the secret of his dormant powers in order to fight opposing forces to a standstill.

When the basic plot idea of *Time War* first occurred to me, I could see at once that the situation and development of the story were and would have to be typically van Vogtian. I resisted the impulse to produce a story that was a pastiche of his style, but in vain. After several false starts had to be abandoned, I knew there was no use in trying to fight against it. The book *wanted* to be a van Vogt puzzle-yarn, and that's the way it had to be written.

I might have stubbornly held out against the irresistible impulse a bit longer, I suppose. But the factor which finally decided me was the knowledge that I would not be the first science fiction writer to "do a van Vogt." For several of my colleagues have already anticipated me and have published van Vogtian pastiches of their own. And excellent ones, too: any knowledgeable reader experienced in the field will probably be able to remember a few examples of his own. But I am thinking in particular of two splendid books: *Flight into Yesterday*, by Charles L. Harness, which appeared in the magazines in 1949 and was published in book form in 1953, and Damon Knight's exciting and suspenseful novel *Beyond the Barrier*, which appeared as a magazine serial in 1963 and came out in hardcovers a year later.

I said to myself, "If these guys can do it, why shouldn't I?"

So I did. And you hold the result in your hands.

So . . . let *Time War* stand as a respectful and affectionate tribute to one of the best and most deservedly popular of all the many fine writers in science fiction's first Golden Age: to A. E. van Vogt, who helped to make it Golden.

—LIN CARTER

Hollis, Long Island, New York